FIRE AND WATER

Hearing the sounds of the battle raging overhead, Eric and Tracy ran down the ship's main corridor leading to the stairs. They climbed to the top, and Eric reached for the doorknob just as an explosion thundered outside. The ship tilted to the right, slamming Eric into Tracy and both of them into the wall. As they scrambled to their feet, bracing themselves on the rocking walls, they heard the clunking sound of hunks of debris raining on deck. A man's pitiful scream mixed with a loud whooshing sound.

"What's going on?" Tracy asked.

"Only one way to find out," Eric said, pulling open the door.

The *Home Run*'s deck was a dense jungle of flames. . . .

THE
WARLORD #2
THE CUTTHROAT
BY JASON FROST

ZEBRA BOOKS
KENSINGTON PUBLISHING CORP.

ZEBRA BOOKS

are published by

KENSINGTON PUBLISHING CORP.
475 Park Avenue South
New York, N.Y. 10016

First printing: January, 1984

Printed in the United States of America

To Sandy Watt,
the world's greatest agent
with the world's saddest cats.

cutthroat *n* one likely to cut throats: murderer *adj* characterized by each player playing for himself rather than having a permanent partner

—*Webster's Third New International Dictionary*

Book One:

ON THE SEA

Tell me, Muse, of the man of many resources who wandered far and wide . . . and on the sea he suffered in his heart many woes.

—Homer

1.

"Duck!"

"Huh?"

"Get your head down!"

She looked around in the dark. Saw nothing. "Why? I don't see—"

Tracy Ammes felt the sharp jolt of Eric's strong hands shoving her roughly off the wooden seat and onto the wet floor of the canoe. She sprawled head first into their nylon backpacks, colliding with such impact that the narrow canoe began to rock furiously, tipping over far enough to scoop great gulps of water over the rails. The black saltwater bounced around inside, soaking the backside of Tracy's tattered jeans.

"Son of a bitch," she sputtered, inching her hands along either side of the canoe's gunwales as she pulled herself upright. "What the hell are you doing? You got me all wet."

"Keep your head down," Eric Ravensmith

repeated urgently, then turned and leaned over the stern of the canoe. He poked his paddle at something out in the water. She couldn't see what.

"You're getting weird, Eric."

No response. His paddle thumped something solid.

"You hear me? *Weird.* Like Tony Perkins or something."

She watched him continue to grapple with whatever he'd found. Something about his intensity frightened her. Eric wasn't the kind of man who spooked easily. In fact, she'd noticed that the more threatening the situation, the calmer he often got, almost icy, like he'd flipped some internal switch that shut down his emotions. That's when he was the most dangerous.

She leaned over the side, trying to see what he was fooling with. No use. Too damn dark.

Tracy swatted at the cold water soaking through her pants. To hell with his overprotectiveness for once. She wasn't little Dorothy from Kansas, he wasn't the goddamned Wizard, and this sure wasn't Oz.

"There's no place like home," she muttered angrily.

"What?"

"Nothing." With a huff she settled her wet butt back on the wooden thwart and massaged her sore knees. They had started to seriously cramp twenty minutes ago and during the last ten minutes they'd gone numb. Not used to the constant kneeling that went along with paddling, she'd taken a break a couple of minutes ago, hauling herself onto the narrow seat and stretching her numb legs. "Stupid canoe," she had complained to Eric. "No wonder the Indians lost. After paddling all day in one of these things they probably couldn't even walk straight."

Then Eric's harsh warning. A brusque shove. Wet butt.

Tracy took a deep breath, calming herself. She'd just been sitting there, nibbling on their last scrawny carrot, which she'd been saving for two days. Testing her discipline. Eric's shove had knocked the carrot out of her hand, but she'd be damned if she wasn't going to sit straight up, head high, and finish every bite of it to spite him. Tracy looked around the canoe for the carrot, squinting through the dark, her hands groping along the five inches of greasy water now swishing in the canoe's bottom. Her thumb bumped something. Quickly, she snatched it up, wiped it on her hooded sweat shirt, and took a loud bite. Salty, but good.

"No noise," Eric whispered sharply.

"Christ, Eric. We're in the middle of the ocean."

"Shhh."

She quietly mashed the half-chewed carrot with her tongue, wondering if she should swallow or spit it out. For a moment she considered hacking it up and spitting it onto his back like a chaw of tobacco. She decided against

11

it. Any other time Eric might have laughed at the idea. But not now.

She heard a splash and Eric's mumbled curse. Though he sat only a few feet away, she could barely make him out in the dense darkness. Since electrical lights were extremely rare anymore, the nights had taken on an ominous blackness she'd not known since she was thirteen, sneaking into the drive-in theater in the trunk of her cousin's Nova to see Connie Francis in *Where the Boys Are*. Now it was as if all the survivors in California were living inside a closed trunk. Shadows seemed coiled in the darkness, somehow blacker and more threatening. The night looked impenetrable. The only lights came from the scattered campfires that speckled the land like distant flickering fireflies.

She looked over the side of the canoe at the soupy black water. They were far away from land now . . . if you didn't count the fact that what used to be one of Huntington Beach's busiest streets was lying eighty feet directly beneath them. Billions of gallons of salt water were tasting land for the first time. Liking it. The surf shops, T-shirt stores, burger stands, and cheap bars, all hunkered under them like a sleazy Atlantis. No lights there.

Overhead the stars and moon offered some faint illumination, but most of it was blocked by the thick Long Beach Halo which curved over the island of California like an inverted salad bowl. Months ago it had transformed the sparkling heavens into a random series of dim

12

smudges. Eric had once said that it reminded him of a sloppy child's fingerpainting.

"Just what the hell am I ducking from?" Tracy finally demanded, sitting even straighter. She felt unreasonable, but couldn't stop herself. Fear brought out her anger. "I don't see anything out there."

Eric answered without looking up. "By the time you did, it would be too late."

"Screw you, Captain Bligh. We haven't seen another human being in two days, not since we launched this Natty Bumpo contraption of yours. What makes you think we're in danger now?"

Eric was half hanging over the stern of the canoe, his broad muscular shoulders hooded like a cobra as they flexed against some weight in the water. Even here, even now, she felt a warm rush of desire for him. For once she fought it.

"I love talking to your back, Eric."

"Good, it's been lonely for conversation."

"What are you fussing with back there?"

He didn't answer.

"Need help?" Sarcastic.

"Yeah. I need you to keep your head down."

She crunched her carrot loudly in response.

Eric, still struggling with something heavy in the water, paused, glanced over his shoulder at Tracy. "I mean it, Trace. Head down. Something's not right here."

What little light there was in the night air seemed immediately drawn to Eric's glacial

13

face, flaring along the thin twisting scar that climbed out of his shirt collar, up his long neck, along the curve of his boxy jaw, then exploding in a round patch on his cheek. The pattern resembled the sparking of a fuse.

Tracy had known him for months, since before the disasters and afterward at the survivor's camp where they'd made him Warlord. Before he lost everything he'd loved. She was used to seeing the scar. Mostly she found it sexy, exotic. It gave off an aura of danger that spiced his rawboned good looks. Some days in some lights you couldn't even see it. Yet other times its intensity still startled her, the way it seemed to almost pulse with life like a winding strip of plastic explosive pasted along his face. The threat of violence lurking beneath the smooth surface skin.

Did he know the image he projected—tough, hard-nosed, ruthless—and how at odds that was with the other sides of him she'd come to know? Like last week when he'd recounted the last battle of the War of the Roses—Bosworth— where Henry Tudor finally defeated and killed Richard III in 1485. Describing all this while scraping out the slimy intestines of a rabbit he'd caught bare-handed and was about to cook with plants he'd dug up that looked suspiciously like weeds to her, but were, he claimed, herbs used by the Hopi Indians. This was also the same man who yelled at her to keep up with him, then slowed down so that she could.

Tracy saw all that in his scar. Even more

14

important, it reminded her how he got it and she felt a shiver run up her spine on tiny clawed feet. It also reminded her of where they were going now—and why. Again the fear yanked at her stomach. But she didn't want Eric to see it.

"I hope all that strain back there is at least for something to eat."

"I don't think we'll eat it just yet," Eric said. "In a few months we may not have a choice."

"What's that supposed to mean?"

He didn't answer. His eyes were lost in the dark like moon craters so she couldn't read his expression.

"Well, if it's not food, what is it?"

"An answer to your question."

"What question?"

He turned back to the object he was wrestling out of the water. The canoe began to rock again from the added weight. "It's snagged on some seaweed."

Tracy braced her hands on either rail of the canoe, shifting her weight back and forth along the seat to maintain their balance. "What question, damn it?"

Eric grunted, heaving his arms up. His catch bobbed partially out of the water.

"*Oh God!*" Tracy gasped, dropping the stub of her carrot again. "*Jesus no!*"

2.

The seventy-three-foot staysail schooner rocked silently in the gentle current only a quarter of a mile ahead of Eric and Tracy's canoe. The heavy darkness completely curtained it from sight and being downwind drowned any sounds. On board, the ship's armed crew stood solemnly on deck, scratching their bodies and fidgeting with their weapons. Waiting and listening.

"What the hell are they doing?" the captain whispered, annoyed. A faint scent of English Leather soap and Polo cologne misted the air around him.

"We could be on them like a bad rash in just five minutes," Griffin urged the captain in his slow Carolina drawl. "Just say the word, Cap."

The captain didn't answer.

"Be over in no time," Griffin pressed. "They'll think their worst nightmare just came true, Cap. They'll be pissing out their guts like the others."

"No," the captain said. "Not yet. Wait until they're closer."

Griffin nodded, forgetting that it was too dark for the captain to see him. He'd learned when not to push it with the Cap. His hands clenched and unclenched around the wooden grip of his bow, which he called The Enforcer after his favorite Clint Eastwood movie. His thumb brushed the tiny nick where he'd blocked a knife thrust a couple weeks ago when they'd hit that tent town up the coast. You have to watch the old folks the most, he thought sagely, especially old ladies. They've always got a knife or a fork or something sharp hidden away on their wrinkled bodies, tucked in their size fifty-four bras or something. That last bitch had stabbed poor dumb Brian Fields to death before Griffin had finally crushed her skull with an Underwood typewriter she'd been sitting at when they'd surprised her. Writing fucking poetry, of all things. Well, he'd warned Brian about geezers. Afterward Griffin had stripped both Brian and the old woman clean. And, after scraping off a hunk of the woman's bloody scalp with Brian's knife, he'd taken the type-writer too. He'd traded the whole lot for a jar of Smucker's strawberry jam and a few cartridges.

"I hear his paddle messing in the water, Cap, but they ain't getting any closer. Maybe it's just kids foolin' around."

"Maybe," the captain said. "And maybe it's Alabaster."

Griffin shrugged, his calloused finger pressing the arrow tight against the bowstring. He was ready, whether it was kids or dogs or Alabaster or Farrah fucking Fawcett. Made no difference to him. Or The Enforcer.

He scratched the blue tattoo etched in the back of his hand. He'd had it done six years ago in Miami after he quit the Coast Guard and joined the merchant marine. The old fart who'd done it had the worst breath he'd ever smelled, like something real sick had crawled in his mouth to die. Still, he'd known his way around a tattoo machine and, despite the thick bifocals, had a steady hand. Griffin loved that tattoo more than he'd ever loved anything or anyone in his life. He figured it said more about him than any amount of talk could. It was a pair of tumbling dice with two words underneath: *No Regrets.*

It itched again. A medical impossibility, the captain, who seemed to know a lot about everything, had often explained. But the sucker itched just the same. Always did before a battle. Like it was anxious to get started.

The ship swayed but made no noise. No creaking or moaning. It was a damn fine ship, better than he'd ever have gotten to sail aboard if it hadn't been for the quakes. She'd sail up the asshole of a hurricane and out again without rustling a hair on the ocean's ass. Whatever craft was floating toward them now, whoever was aboard, they didn't have a chance against this baby.

19

Not to mention this crew. Griffin had sailed with strange crews before, but this one won the Grand Prize at the Looney Tunes Festival. Fucking maniacs. When they weren't grabbing at each others privates—no matter what the sex—they were stealing from each other or fighting over skin magazines. That was one thing he could say about himself, he hadn't turned fruity or bi-fucking-sexual.

Griffin reached back and smoothed his long ponytail. It was the only hair on his head, sprouting from the crown of his skull amidst a desert of bare skin like a rooster's tail. If only his old ballbusting Coast Guard captain, T.J. Phelps, could see him now. Or his folks back in Greensboro, for Chrissakes. They'd shit barbed wire. He stroked the ponytail as if it were a pet, then ran his rough hands over his bald head. He'd modeled the style after that guy on *Kung Fu* he used to watch while in the Guard. Wanted one ever since. That was another great thing about the quakes, you could be anything you wanted now. Funny thing was, on this ship, he was one of the more normal-looking bastards.

They listened silently for a few minutes. Behind them was the slight trickling sound of someone pissing overboard. Griffin sighed, maneuvered across the dark deck until he was near the culprit. "Stick it back in your pants right now, Devon, before I cut it off." The immediate sound of a zipper hastily tugged shut.

Griffin rejoined the captain. They could hear

the distant voice skipping like a flat stone across the placid ocean. It was a woman's voice. Good, Griffin grinned. Very good. She sounded frightened about something out there. He chuckled, tapped his finger against The Enforcer. She'd be better off worrying about what's waiting out here.

"They've found something, Cap," he said.

"I *know* that," the captain hissed, snapping the thick rubber band he always wore around his wrist.

A bad sign, Griffin realized. Usually meant he was getting angry, starting to lose it again. Christ, he hoped not. Not yet. Not until this was over. The captain was the only thing that kept this crew from killing each other. And he was already scary enough without one of his fucking spells. At least in the dark he didn't have to look at Cap's face. There was no getting used to that sight.

Something splashed in the water.

"They're moving," Griffin said, slipping quietly toward the stern of the ship. It wouldn't be wise to be right next to Cap when the action started. Besides, that was *her* job. He looked around deck, couldn't see her, but knew she was standing nearby. She always was. She was the only woman he'd ever met who really scared him. Cap and her were two of a kind.

As Griffin eased across the ship's deck, he heard the thick rubber band snap twice. A very bad sign . . .

. . . for whoever was out there.

3.

"Please, Eric, get rid of it," Tracy pleaded.

Eric's hands were clutching the lapels of a sopping denim jacket. Inside the jacket slumped the bloated body of a young man in his early twenties. Water lapped his chest as he bobbed next to the canoe. Exact age was hard to determine because the skin was so puffy with water. Rubbery, like moist bread dough. Parts of the face had been nibbled away by fish, particularly the lips and the right side of the mouth all the way back to the cheekbone. The clenched teeth that showed through the flapping flesh hinted at the grinning skeleton lurking beneath.

But Eric's purpose in hauling him out of the water to show her was clear now. So was his warning. A wooden arrow had drilled through the face just to the left of the nose and was sticking out the back of the skull.

"Seen enough?"

She nodded, unable to work her frozen mouth.

Eric wrapped his fingers around the wooden arrow and firmly tugged. The shaft moved slowly at first, reluctant.

"What the hell are you doing?" Tracy asked, horrified.

"We may need the arrow." He added a little more muscle, twisting the arrow as he pulled. Finally it dislodged from the skull. The soggy skin tore easily, clinging to the wood like wet tissue paper. Eric swirled the shaft in the water a few times, rinsing it clean, then handed it to Tracy. "Put it in your quiver with the others."

She held the arrow, said nothing.

Eric pushed the dead man away from the canoe and wiped his hands on the thighs of his Levis. They watched the boy's lifeless arms flop into the water, the swollen body rotate face down with black water bubbling like a fountain through the hole in the back of his head.

"*That's* why you keep your head down," Eric said, kneeling back down and grabbing his paddle. "Understand?"

Tracy tucked the arrow into her quiver next to the long bow, fighting the surge of nausea clawing in her stomach. Her mouth tasted bitter, metallic, as if she'd been sucking a rusty nail. Fresh blood. Sometime within the last minute she'd bit her lower lip. She prodded the

24

wound with her tongue, then ignored it. She fished the fallen carrot stub from the canoe and finished the last two bites.

Since Atlas and Thor—that's what the outside world called the great earthquakes that had instantly made obsolete every map and globe in the world—Tracy had seen her share of horrors, ghastly sights much worse than that boy's chewed-up face. It wasn't merely his bloated corpse which was making her feel so chilled and sick, it was the constant unexpectedness of it all. Living in a perpetual state of tension, of being on guard. Like an unending Tunnel of Terror ride in a carnival. Peek around any corner, open any door, turn over any rock and you might suddenly be looking down the barrel of a madman's shotgun or staring at a mutilated body. Or worse. In this new world, the flesh had lost all dignity.

Tracy grabbed an empty Campbell's Tomato Rice soup can Eric had tied to the thwart, and began bailing water out of the canoe.

She kept her head tucked low.

Eric was kneeling in the stern, facing her, paddling with slow powerful strokes. Occasionally he would change sides or let the blade of the paddle drag so he could steer. Each stroke dug into the slick black water without a sound, propelling them along as smoothly as if they were sliding across glass.

Tracy tossed another canful of icy water over the side, then looked up. "Eric?"

"Yeah?"

"Do you think Goldie Hawn's still alive?"

"Huh?"

"I've been kinda wondering, you know, if maybe Goldie Hawn was killed in the quake. I know it's crazy. But I've been thinking about it a lot lately. Like maybe she was home with her kids. Or maybe she was somewhere on location, safe. Don't ask me why her, I'm not even that much of a fan."

Eric smiled.

"I just hope we don't come across her corpse like all the others." She stared at him, her eyes intent. "You think I'm nuts, right?"

"Nope. For a while at the beginning, I used to wonder the same thing about Pavarotti. And I hate opera." He shrugged. "Trick of the mind, I guess. We miss the things we never got a chance to know. Even if we didn't like something, it was still there, so we might like it someday. Taps into our sense of hope."

"Like New Yorkers who've never been to the top of the Empire State Building. At least they knew they *could* go."

"Right."

"Hey! Maybe in a couple months we can start a gossip magazine. A *Who's Who* of celebrity survivors."

The canoe sliced quietly through the water.

"Eric?"

"Yeah?"

"I hate boats. That's why I've been acting

strange lately."

"I noticed."

"You've never complained. Not once."

"Is that an accusation?"

"No. Well, yes. You make me feel so damn guilty. Always patient and understanding. You rehearsing for sainthood?"

He laughed. "No, I figured it was just withdrawal tension, you know, from quitting smoking."

"I never smoked."

"Really?" He shrugged. "My mistake."

Tracy laughed, her first in the two weeks since Eric had revealed his plan for them to take to the sea. The news had reached out, grabbed her by the throat, and had been squeezing tighter ever since. Not only did she hate boats, she hated any kind of water that didn't come out of a tap or was safely enclosed in a pool. *Jaws* had only confirmed her worst fears about the sea, begun when she was a child watching Disney's *20,000 Leagues Under the Sea*. For weeks afterward she'd suspected a giant squid lived inside the toilet, waiting for her. She used to run next door to the Riker's house to use their bathroom. Once she didn't make it.

But this was even worse, knowing that they were floating over the drowned remnants of cities she used to romp through back in high school. Yesterday Corona del Mar. Today Huntington Beach, where she once dated that surfer her parents hated, Davy Lee. Silver

Surfer, his buddies had called him. Was Davy down there now, hanging upside down from the ankle strap attached to his surfboard while fish gnawed away the cute dimples she'd loved to kiss when she was sixteen?

Eric was doing his best to make her feel better, letting her blow off steam without comment. It made her feel like a selfish child. After all, he had lost more than she, had even more to lose if they didn't hurry. So even under his cheerful patter she could detect the grim determination in his eyes.

But he hadn't always been so calm and understanding. She still remembered the rage that had fueled him only a few weeks ago during all that killing at Savvytown. Suddenly she realized that he had not dragged that murdered body out of the water just to prove to her there might be danger or to retrieve an arrow. He had wanted to study the face. Make sure it wasn't *him*. Dirk Fallows.

"Eric, are you sure Fallows came this way?"

"You were there when I questioned that old man in Anaheim. He said a white-haired man in his forties and a young boy. Described Fallows and Timmy perfectly. Said the man shot him before stealing his boat. That's Fallows' style."

"Except that the old man lived."

"Fallows wanted him to. So he could tell us."

"Okay, but he could have taken that boat in any direction."

28

"No, he'd—" Eric paused, peered into the dark, looked troubled.

"What's wrong?"

"Shhh." He stopped paddling, tilted his ear to the wind.

Tracy listened, heard nothing. Same old shrill wind.

After a few minutes of listening, Eric began paddling again.

"What's wrong?"

"Wind sounded funny, as if it had to shift around some large object."

"Like an island?"

"Maybe. Or some debris. Could be anything."

Silently she peered into the night, unable to distinguish anything in the foggy darkness. The sea and air seemed one solid seamless black mass. They might as well be paddling underwater.

Eric continued speaking as if there had been no interruption, but Tracy could see him tilting his head for sound, still listening. He pulled his crossbow closer. "I figure Fallows stole the boat and took Timmy up to join his troops in Santa Barbara."

"Think he knows we're following?"

"He's counting on it. He just doesn't know we'd also come by boat. Probably figures to beat us there by a couple days. Get his men ready. They'll be waiting for us."

Tracy scraped the soup can along the bottom of the canoe, scooping up the last of the water

29

and dumping it over the side. "That leaves me with only one question."

"I know. What was that boy's body doing out here this far from shore with an arrow through his face and no boat?"

"Right."

"Well, he wasn't keeping his head down, that's for sure."

"Do you think he was—"

Eric's ears perked. He stopped paddling and swiveled his head to the left.

Suddenly an explosion of blinding light stabbed their eyes.

A deep voice echoed across the water. "Ahoy there, maties," it said in an amused, cynical tone.

The large ship had been waiting dead in the water, cloaked by the darkness and silence. As soon as Tracy and Eric had come within fifty yards, someone on board had switched on a high-beam searchlight. The bright white tunneled through the dark, flooding over the canoe like a vaudeville spotlight. Eric and Tracy shielded their eyes, but they still could not see the ship clearly. Only that it loomed behind the light like a large dark building. And that it was close.

"Let me see," the voice said. "What's the best way to put this without sounding, um, insensitive?"

Jeering laughter from the crew.

The captain continued, enjoying his own

30

cleverness. "I've got it. Adds just the right touch of melodrama." This time the voice was humorless, hard and cold. "How about, *surrender or die!*"

The crew hooted obscene approval.

Eric reached for his crossbow.

4.

Eric's hand grazed the cool metal stock of the crossbow, but he didn't lift it into sight. The glaring searchlight from the ship made him feel too exposed, like a grasshopper impaled on a pin.

"What do you want?" he shouted at the ship.

"Want?" The voice affected a tone of surprise. "Fellowship, my dear man. The love of a good woman. Perhaps two. The respect of my peers. To die in bed at age ninety-nine, humping twin sixteen-year-old virgins."

Howling laughter from the crew.

"I want whatever I can *take*," he barked angrily. A match flared behind the searchlight, briefly outlining a broad lump of a man. The red tip of a cigarette glowed. The gesture was not lost on Eric. Cigarettes were a habit only of the powerful. Two cigarettes could buy you a horse. Three a whole town.

Eric glanced over at Tracy. She was quietly

working her Colt Cobra .38 out of the nylon backpack. There were only three bullets left in the cylinder, their last three. He watched her pale hands trembling as she stared directly into the blinding light. Her expression was tense, yet defiant. She fidgeted with the gun in her lap, finally easing the safety off.

"We don't have anything of value," Eric called. "A few cans of food, a couple canteens of water."

"Food and water, huh?"

"Yeah. And the canoe."

"That's all?"

"That's all."

The captain snickered. "Surely you under-estimate the worth of your cargo, my friend. From here you look absolutely laden with treasure."

Eric's hand tightened around the crossbow's black stock, dragging it across the curved ribs of the canoe. His finger snuggled against the cold trigger and he noticed for the first time that his hands were sweating. Good, he liked to be a little frightened. It kept him from doing anything stupid. He pulled the bow closer. Already cocked and armed with a sharp wooden bolt, the waxed string strained to flex its one hundred seventy-five pounds of pressure against the arrow.

"Quite the charmer," Tracy said. Her voice was flat, almost dreamy as she stared into the light.

"David Niven he ain't."

"The Welcome Wagon he ain't, either." She clenched her fist tighter around the gun.

"Easy," Eric soothed.

She didn't answer.

"Trace?"

"I'm fine," she said, but Eric could see that she wasn't.

It wasn't just the danger of their situation that was frightening Tracy now. The threatening tone of the man's voice had been oily with innuendo. His references to her as a "treasure" were not meant to flatter, merely assess, as one might livestock, for sale. Or cargo.

The quakes that had ripped California from the rest of the continent, that had sent a billowing dome of chemical and biological weapons clouding the sky to cut them off from the rest of the world, had also brought a lot of social changes among the survivors. People, who before had felt only marginally bound by society's rules, now felt free to do whatever they wanted. Whatever the cost. A few had turned their ruthlessness into profit, selling, whatever was in short supply. The millions of deaths in the quakes and subsequent fires had left a lot of severe shortages: food, water, weapons—and one that the survivalist magazines hadn't predicted. Women.

And business abhors a vacuum.

So women soon became good business. Scavenging entrepreneurs created an underground slave trade in women, sometimes buying them from camps, sometimes stealing them.

A settlement of men might chip in a whole case of Heinz baked beans for a healthy woman. And if she was a little attractive, they might be willing to toss in an additional case of plums in extra heavy syrup.

"Now, I want you both to sit perfectly still," the captain ordered. "A couple of my men will be over to, um, welcome you."

Eric did not respond.

"Did you hear me?"

Eric studied Tracy in the bright beam that washed over her face. Last week she'd insisted he hack off her wavy red hair with his knife until it was as short as his. Now it wreathed her head in wispy tufts like the furry red petals of some exotic flower. True, it was easier to keep clean, and under some circumstances might allow her to pass for a male, but still he'd hated doing it. Not just because it had been so stunningly beautiful before, but for a much more selfish reason. One that he'd felt too guilty to admit. Her hair reminded him of Annie, his murdered wife.

Sometimes while lying in Tracy's arms, Eric would wrap her thick long hair around his fist, between his fingers, the way he used to do with Annie's. And for a few precious moments he would be back in their quiet suburban home. Timmy and Jenny would be playing chess, Jenny with one ear cocked for telephone calls from boys. He and Annie would be cuddling on the sofa, watching a video-tape movie they'd rented. The history professor and his family.

Happily average, his infamous past almost forgotten.

But that was before.

Before the quakes. Before his daughter's throat had been slit open. Before Annie's neck had been snapped. Before his son, Timmy, had been stolen.

Before Dirk Fallows had returned.

Sometimes Eric wasn't sure whether his fondness for Tracy was for who she was or because she reminded him of Annie. He suspected Tracy knew this. Perhaps that was why she'd suddenly insisted on having her hair cut off.

He wasn't sorry he'd taken up with her so soon after Annie's death. This new world was unforgiving and impatient, allowed no time for mourning. Not if you were to survive.

Looking at her attractive angular features now, he couldn't imagine anyone mistaking her for a man. If anything the ragged haircut made her look even sexier, perhaps in the way it emphasized her beauty while hinting at the toughness underneath. A smooth stream sliding over sharp stones.

"We're not going to have any trouble from you, are we?" the captain asked lazily.

"We don't want trouble," Eric shouted back.

"Nor do we. But you've got trouble, my friend. Right here in River City." He chuckled. "And unless the two of you follow my orders, your trouble is spelled with a capital T which rhymes with D which stands for dead. Should I sing you a stanza?"

Eric didn't answer. No point, the guy was too full of his own wit, chattering away with manic energy.

"Griffin!"

"Cap?" someone on board answered.

"We've had a request. Play your instrument for the lovely couple. Something romantic."

Instantly Eric heard the unmistakable sound of a bow string snapping. An arrow thwacked wood, poked through the canvas and splintered a rib of the canoe's hull. The sharp metal tip lodged only inches away from Eric's knees.

Bravo!" the captain said, applauding. Others on board joined in the applause, whistling and jeering. "A virtuoso performance, wouldn't you agree? You might even say he handles a bow better than Isaac Stern, eh?" The captain cackled with laughter.

Eric lifted the crossbow to his lap, waited.

"Apparently you two lack a sense of humor." The captain's voice hardened, shouting across the water now as if enraged. "You *will* remain motionless while my men approach you."

Out of the dark shadows skirting the ship, a small dinghy emerged. One man rowed, the other sat on the rear transom with a 9-mm Uzi submachine gun aimed at Eric and Tracy.

Somewhere in the dark Eric thought he heard a rubber band snapping.

"We'd prefer not to waste any precious bullets on you, so your cooperation will be appreciated." The captain's voice was calmer now, but measured, as if he was still struggling to control his temper. "By the way, you do have the Alabaster map, don't you?"

"The what?" Eric asked.

There was a pause. Eric heard the buzzing of whispered conversation. A woman's shrill voice mingled with the man's.

"No matter," the captain said cheerfully. He flicked the cigarette overboard in a bright arc of red light. "Perhaps you will feel more like talking on board. If not, well, we shall make do."

The dark figure behind the spotlight walked across the ship's deck, his thick body outlined in the rim of white from the searchlight. Then he was gone. Another figure, shorter, thinner, took his place behind the light.

The rowboat glided closer. The only sound was the oars pounding water with a quick cadence.

Tracy lifted the Colt .38 from her lap.

"Wait," Eric whispered.

"For what?"

"Wait."

She hesitated, then rested the gun back on her lap. She rolled her lower lip between her teeth, bit lightly.

The rowboat sliced through the black water until it too was basking in the bright beam from the ship's searchlight. The oarsman's back was to the canoe, but he kept looking over his shoulder at Tracy.

"Eric, look," she pointed.

Eric stared at the approaching men. Both looked like refugees from the midnight screening he'd attended last June of *The Rocky Horror Picture Show*. Annie had dressed in an outrageous costume, sneaking past the baby-sitter and children. Stripping out of her trench-coat in the car, she'd swiveled the rearview mirror over so she could shovel on her makeup while he drove. They'd laughed all the way to the theater.

But these men were serious. Their faces were caked white with some kind of makeup. Thick black mascara rimmed their eyes, scarlet lipstick was smeared on their lips. The oarsman's greasy hair was knotted into a heavy braid that hung down the middle of his muscular back like black rope. The skinny gunman on the transom wore an expensive black tuxedo with no shirt underneath, just his pale bumpy chest. Around his bony neck he wore a white flea collar.

"Jesus," Tracy said.

"Get ready."

"For what?"

"All the gear tied down?"

"Yeah."

"I mean everything. Backpacks, weapons."

She looked at him, realizing. "Oh no, Eric."

He lashed the paddles to the thwarts, secured the extra bolts for his bow in one of the backpacks.

"There's got to be another way."

"You think of one?"

The rowboat splashed closer. The gunman

40

with the flea collar stood up in the boat and waved his Uzi. "Shut the fuck up, assholes."

The oarsman glanced over his huge shoulder and leered at Tracy. Three of his front teeth were missing. The others looked like rotten prunes.

Tracy sighed at Eric and shrugged resignation.

"Keep your head down," Eric winked.

"I said to shut up!" the gunman screamed. The rowboat was only ten feet away now, directly between the canoe and the ship. "You want to suck on the end of this, jerkoff?" He waved the Uzi at Eric.

Tracy snapped up her Colt in a double-fisted grip and fired. The .38 slug blasted a hole through the gunman's wrist, splashing a pattern of blood on the tuxedo jacket and bare skin of his chest. Undaunted, the bullet continued on through the wrist and into the center of the bloody pattern, burrowing another hole through his bony chest. The impact flipped him over the side of the small boat. His heavy boots dragged his dying body to the sunken sidewalks of Huntington Beach below.

The oarsman grabbed at his partner's Uzi, which had clattered to the floor of the rowboat. He had it in an instant and was swinging toward the canoe.

Eric hefted his Barnett Commando crossbow to waist level and pulled the trigger. The bolt jumped out of the bow, plunging through the oarsman's red Linda Ronstadt T-shirt. The Uzi dropped from his hand into the boat, but he didn't seem to care. He sat back down with a heavy thud, staring blandly at the feathered plume lodged in his chest. Blood even redder than his lipstick oozed out of the corner of his mouth.

"Kill them!" a woman's voice commanded. It was high-pitched, unmistakably Oriental. For a second, Eric thought he recognized it.

A submachine gun flared on the ship and a dozen bullets chewed through the rowboat and across the legs of the oarsman before one finally rammed through the canoe. The oarsman didn't scream, just looked confused, his heavy-lidded stare still fixed on the protruding arrow.

"Move!" Eric hollered at Tracy, and both threw themselves backward over the side of the canoe. Eric held on to the gunwale, purposely tipping the canoe over with him.

Under the black saltwater he couldn't see anything but the rim of light above that outlined the overturned canoe. He reached his arms out, flailing to find Tracy. His fingers grazed her head and he fought to get a grip on her short hair, yanking her up next to him. He knew she was a fine swimmer, but he also knew the terror even good swimmers feel when thrown into a dark ocean at night. He'd seen experienced soldiers become unhinged as they thought about all the primitive life teeming around them searching for food.

They bobbed up directly under the over-turned canoe. Two rods of light slanted through the dark where the searchlight lit the bullet holes.

"Just tread here for a while," he said. "There's plenty of air and they'll probably think we swam away."

Tracy sputtered water, nodded weakly.

"No bullets!" the woman's clipped oriental voice screeched from the ship. "Save bullets."

"What the hell's going on?" the captain's voice challenged; apparently he was returning from below deck.

Their voices became quiet for a minute.

"How long should we stay?" Tracy whispered.

"We'll let the current carry us away. They must have a pretty big ship, not all that easy to maneuver in the dark, even with their searchlights. Besides it would take them a while to haul all the sails up."

"They could use the motor."

"Providing they have any fuel and are willing to waste it on us." He shook his head as he secured his crossbow to the thwarts. "Nope, my guess is they'll just write us off and sit it out for the rest of the night."

Three arrows slammed through the side of the canoe. One of them plowed a couple inches of skin from Eric's neck. He felt the sting of saltwater splashing his bleeding wound.

"Down!" he barked, pushing Tracy's head underwater as he dove under after her. They came up on the outside of the canoe, their heads

43

still hidden from the ship. Another volley of arrows whistled through the air, some piercing the canoe, others splashing in the water around them like crazy fish.

"We swim?" Tracy asked, her teeth chattering from the cold water.

"Yeah. We swim."

"Which way?"

He pointed.

"Eric, that's *toward* their ship!"

"Right. They've got their light searching all over the water. They're bound to find us when we come up for air. Unless we're where they aren't looking."

"Like in their laps?"

Half a dozen arrows slammed into the canoe, another half a dozen sliced through the water.

"Damn," Tracy said, "I just felt one graze my sneaker."

"How long can you hold your breath?" Eric asked.

"As long as I have to, I guess."

"Good. We won't be able to see each other underwater, so grab hold of the waistband of my pants once we're underwater."

"My boyfriend in high school already tried that line."

Eric smiled, wishing for a moment he could see her more clearly. Just in case they didn't make it. He pulled her toward him, found her shivering lips with his own. Kissed. Salty tongues flicked against each other. It was over in a second, but it gave both strength. "Take

44

some deep breaths, force the air down. Your lungs only operate at a third their capacity during normal breathing." She sucked the air deep into her lungs. "Okay, let's go," he said, diving under the water. He waited until Tracy had groped along his back and snagged his waistband before diving deeper, out of lethal range of any stray arrows.

The numbing cold of the water seemed to wring his muscles with each stroke. Occasionally his hand brushed something floating, and he wondered if it was seaweed or a shark or that boy's body he'd dragged up. But he pushed on, scooping water aside as he swam blindly toward the ship, hoping he was still going in the right direction. Hoping that this plan was better than the last one.

After a while he felt that insistent twitching in his chest, the burning spasms of the last of his oxygen being consumed. The muscles in his throat began to flutter, demanding air. Tracy was yanking on his waistband, urging him to go up to the surface. He couldn't be sure of exactly where they were right now, but he was sure that they weren't close enough yet. He kept swimming.

Tracy's tugging became more desperate, panicky. But he swam on, fighting the screaming in his own body. They had to keep going. Finally Tracy let go, pushing off his back and shooting up toward the surface. Eric reached up, grabbed her churning ankle, and yanked her back down, wrapping his arm tightly around her chest. She fought weakly as he pulled her through the water. Just a few more yards, he thought, kicking furiously.

He heard the sudden rush of bubbles escape from her mouth, felt her chest convulse as it gulped water. She was drowning.

He had no choice now. He broke for surface.

5.

Vomit and saltwater bubbled from Tracy's mouth.

Eric flipped her over in the water so she wouldn't choke, letting the fluids drain from her mouth. Rivulets of black water and mucus gushed from her nostrils. Her eyes rolled up into her head, her eyelids fluttering.

"C'mon, damn it. Breathe." He gripped her tight with one arm, pressing his fist between her shoulder blades. A stream of soupy liquid pumped from her mouth. The growl of her retching echoed loudly across the dark water.

She sucked air, coughed. Breathed.

"Over there," someone shouted. The searchlight swiveled noisily on rusty hinges and Eric saw the saucer of light skimming over the surface of the water toward them.

"There. *There!*" the oriental woman's voice directed.

Eric looked up, saw the huge ship rocking

only a dozen yards away. A few more seconds and he'd have made it to safety. But Tracy wouldn't have.

He squinted into the glaring searchlight, boosting Tracy afloat with one arm, treading water with the other. He stared at the ship and calculated his options for escape. He found none. The light cast a bright pool of warmth around them that reminded Eric how cold the water was. Tracy's body hung limply in his arms now, but she was still shivering. She half-opened her eyes, looked around sleepily. "Sorry."

"There, there," he said. It was something he used to say to his kids, but he didn't know what else to say. It seemed to calm Tracy. She closed her eyes, squeezed out a tear.

"We've decided to surrender," Eric hollered up to the ship.

An arrow whistled out of the dark, splashed water in front of them, kicking a spray in Eric's face before disappearing underwater. He felt a sudden sharp pressure in his chest where the arrow lodged. A warm tingling spidered out from the wound, crept along his flesh. Tracy floated free from his arms. The water began to rise around him.

"No, Angel!" he heard the captain's voice yell. "Not until we have the fucking map."

Angel. Eric remembered who she was now, the familiar harsh voice from a distant nightmare. Angel. It had been many years. He thought she was dead.

"Eric!" Tracy screamed, grabbing weakly

48

at him.

Too late. The water folded over his head with downy gentleness. Liquid arms carried him through the crowded ocean. Everything was quiet tonight in the thick darkness of Huntington Beach. He was sinking.

6.

Tracy shrugged the rough blanket off her shoulders and stood shivering in her bra and panties. She squeezed the leg of her jeans, the shoulder of her sweat shirt. Damp, but better than standing around naked in a smelly blanket. This way she felt less vulnerable.

She pulled her clothes from the bunk where they'd been drying and climbed into them. The wet denim scraped against her unshaven legs. Not having to shave her legs and armpits was the only advantage of living in California now—the way making a right turn on a red light used to be.

C'mon, Tracy, she scolded herself, don't flip out now.

There was a rustling behind her, a low moan.

"Am I dead?" Eric asked quietly, his eyes opening.

"Too soon to tell."

He grinned, figuring the effect was worth

the pain.

Tracy's cool fingers pressed against his forehead, holding him down. He could have told her he wasn't going anywhere. Not until someone removed the Plymouth from his chest. In a minute or two he'd worry about the situation. Right now he closed his eyes, let the ship's swaying lull him for a moment. He slipped into a dream and saw Annie smiling, waving, her neck twisted at an unnatural angle. Behind her stood Fallows, smirking, holding Timmy's hand. Timmy's mouth curved into an evil leer. Eric forced his eyes back open. His own grin was gone.

He looked down at his chest, recognized the blue cotton material used to bandage his wound. "I see your sweat shirt's missing a hood and some sleeves. You getting into the punk look?"

Tracy snorted. "On this ship who would notice?"

He looked around the cabin. It was a double stateroom with extra sleeping bags lying in twisted heaps on the floor. Enough bedding to sleep an expanded crew. A sloppy crew by the looks of things. Dirty clothes were thrown everywhere, tattered skin magazines spread-eagled on several bunks. Eric turned his head to the wall. Ragged pages torn carelessly from the magazines were tacked to the wall. Naked women. Naked men. Naked boys with girls no more than eleven or twelve.

"How you feeling?" Tracy asked.

"I wish you wouldn't try to sound so chipper. Makes me think I've got only minutes to live."

"Sorry," she said. She wasn't talking about now.

Eric reached out, traced her jawline with his finger. "Forget it. Really."

"Guess I couldn't hold my breath as long as I thought."

He gestured with his chin at the messy stateroom. "If you lived in this room long enough, you'd learn to hold it indefinitely."

It got a slight smile.

Eric struggled to prop himself onto his elbows. A flaming spear skewered his chest.

"Don't move, Eric. Without our clothes from the canoe, I can't afford to lose any more of this sweat jacket to make fresh bandages."

With the sleeves ripped off the jacket, her long smooth arms hung naked to her sides. The skin was tan from weeks of exposure to the sun, the muscles sharply defined from the exercise. A few scabs and scratches in various stages of healing decorated her arms. Broken blisters and callous pads clumped on her palms. Her face remained pale, though Eric thought he noticed a gradual building up of freckles across the bridge of the nose. The nose itself was still a little crooked from a fall from a horse a month ago. To him, she was more beautiful than ever.

Eric walked his fingers across his bandaged chest, probing the sore and tender spots. When they touched the rim of the wound he winced, clenching his face like a fist. "Christ!"

"You were lucky it wasn't worse. The water probably slowed the arrow some. Not to mention your chipped rib."

"Take the bandage off," he said quietly.

"What?"

"Take it off." He swung his legs over the side of the bunk, swallowing the pain. His head pulsed with electrical shocks. He clawed at the jersey bandages, unwinding them.

Tracy clutched his hand, trying to stop him. "What are you doing? You want to bleed to death?"

He shook his head, not wanting to squander his waning energy on words. "Tighter. Make it tighter."

"Okay, okay. Tighter." She grabbed the cloth, began rewinding it, pulling it tighter, watching him swoon under the pressure. "Jeez, Eric . . ." She hesitated.

"Tighter!"

She finished wrapping it. The hard muscles of Eric's chest bulged slightly over the edges of the bandage. The stony ridges of his flat stomach shone with sweat.

He took a deep breath, exhaled slowly. "Good. Now at least I can move."

"Move? Move where?"

"Escape."

"Escape?" She stomped over to the narrow porthole of the cabin, pointed out through the glass. "Unless you're planning to squeeze through there, forget escape. After they fished us out last night, I counted ten men and three women up there. All armed. All who would have trouble deciding which would be more fun, killing you or twisting the legs off a puppy." She spun back to face him. "Get the picture now?"

"Yeah." He stood up, naked. "Where are my clothes?"

She threw up her hands, yanked his still-damp clothes from the bunk where she'd hung them to dry, and threw them at his chest. The impact knocked him back onto the bunk with a groan. "Escape, huh?" She shook her head. "My hero."

Eric dressed slowly, each movement like some elaborate mime. Tracy didn't offer to help him. She stood with her arms crossed staring out the porthole. It was dawn outside, the sun just beginning its ascent somewhere behind the Long Beach Halo. The sky was already the hazy orange yellow color it would remain for the rest of the day. The ship was moving along at a pretty decent clip.

"Did you get a look at our captain?"

"No. He must've been below when they brought us aboard."

"How about the oriental woman?"

"Yeah, she was snapping out a lot of orders, throwing me dirty looks as if I'd stolen her last pair of pantyhose."

"She get a good look at me?"

Tracy laughed. "What balls. I hate to crush your ego, Eric, but she didn't seem interested. Maybe you're not Chinese enough."

"She's not Chinese; she's Vietnamese."

"Whatever." Tracy paused, turned to stare at him. "How do you know? You were unconscious."

"I know her. That's why we've got to escape as soon as possible. I don't know why they didn't kill us last night, but once she sees me, they won't hesitate."

"Why? What'd you do to her?"

He stood up, zipped his pants. "I killed her."

"You what?"

"Or at least I thought I had. Back in 'Nam, when I was with the Night Shift. She'd been selling military secrets to the Cong out of Saigon. Orders came in that she was supposed to disappear. Fallows sent me." He walked over to the porthole, watched the orange-crested waves whip by. Last night they'd been so black and cheerless as they'd closed over him like a coffin lid. "Guess, I blew it. But I know I killed *somebody*."

But who? Who belonged to the body he'd pumped two 7.62-mm sniper slugs into fourteen years ago? Whose arms had flailed in the air, clutching at the wounds before flopping onto the floor of her bedroom, her winter coat buttoned to the neck as she'd prepared to go out at the usual time. He'd framed her face in his scope seconds before pulling the trigger. It *had* been her.

"Just take my word for it, Tracy. We're better off making a run for it than waiting for her to recognize me."

Tracy sat on the edge of the bunk and shook her head. "I don't know."

"You don't know?"

"Yeah. I'm not anxious to be auctioned off to some slimy sex-starved men, Eric. But I'm not sure certain death is better. I want to live."

He nodded. She was right. It was one of the things he liked about Tracy, her practicality. None of that save-the-last-bullet-for-me-rather-than-let-the-Indians-get-me bullshit. She's learned fast. It's better to live. It's always better to live.

But Eric had other considerations. They would definitely kill him; there was no profit to be made in keeping him alive like there was with Tracy. And he had to stay alive. Timmy was still out there, a prisoner of Dirk Fallows. Eric had to do something about both of them.

"Okay," he said. "I'll go on my own. If I make it, I'll try to catch up with you later."

"Sorry, Eric." She shook her head. "Guess I'm saying that a lot lately."

"No need to. In your place I wouldn't risk it either."

The door banged open and a squat thick-necked man jumped into the cabin aiming Eric's crossbow at them. He was shorter than Tracy, but with huge bulging muscles and a nasty sneer. A long ponytail hung like a question mark from his otherwise bald head. A .45 M1911A1 was holstered to his hip.

"Okay, Cap," Griffin said, stepping away from the door to make room.

"Thank you, Griffin," the deep voice intoned as he entered.

Eric stared silently at the captain's face. He thought he'd seen bodies ravaged in every way possible in 'Nam and lately in ways he didn't think were possible in New California. But this sight stunned him, made his stomach tumble. He heard a low moan of panic gurgle in Tracy's throat as she recoiled a few steps, her back pressed to the cabin wall. She gazed fixedly at his face, mesmerized by its grotesqueness.

The left half of the face was almost normal, perhaps once even handsome. But it was the right half that knocked the air out of you. The rough gray skin swirled in thick twisted lumps as if the flesh had once begun to melt, then changed its mind. The heavy brow sagged over the right eye almost blocking it out entirely. Yet under the thick canopy of gnarled skin shone that moist black eye. Intelligent, yet cruel, like some swamp creature's. The crusted mouth twisted into a thin slit that seemed partially frozen, stuck together on the right side. He wore a clean white skipper's cap to complement his flamboyant blue double-breasted blazer, its brass buttons buffed to a high polish. But the head peeking out of the hat was almost bald, flecked with clumps of wispy colorless hair the consistency of parched prairie weeds. The right ear was nothing more than a leathery hole, almost reptilian.

The captain smiled, but only the left half of his mouth moved. "I take it from your stares you

58

don't like my hat?"

Tracy didn't answer, swallowed loudly.

Eric glanced at Griffin, the crossbow pointing at his already damaged chest. No sense in trying anything yet. Wait for an opening.

"Guess you weren't expecting such a natty dresser, eh?" The disfigured captain laughed, the damaged side of his face shifting into islands of wrinkled scars. He looked at Eric. "In the meantime, there's someone *dying* to meet you." He held out a hand like an emcee introducing a new act. "Heeere's Angel."

The slender Vietnamese woman walked into the room. She was short, barely clearing five feet, but her face was just as beautiful as when Eric has last seen it, magnified through the lens of his M-84 scope. The royal tilt of the head, the long black hair cascading around her face. The slits of olive skin encasing eyes gleaming like stainless steel ball bearings. The pouting lips hiding small delicate teeth. But the hate in her face as she stared at Eric was almost as disfiguring as her companion's deformity.

"So, Eric," she said, not smiling, her accent still heavy and halting, "once again you are my guest."

The captain smiled at Eric. "I understand you've already met my little Angel."

"Yes," Angel answered for Eric. "The last time Eric was my guest he made love to me all night. Then tried to kill me in the morning."

"How rude," the man said, clucking his tongue, half of his face crinkled with amusement, the other half a desolate moonscape. "Well, I suppose we will be forced to return the favor, eh, Angel?"

Angel reached behind her back. When her hand reappeared it was clutching a Philippine balisong knife. She flicked her wrist and the double handles unfolded to reveal a sharp blade. She stepped toward Eric.

7.

"Right here." She tapped the point of the blade against Eric's bandaged chest, then pulled the knife away, resting the tip against her pouting lip. Her tongue flicked against the blade absently as she studied his bare torso. When she decided on the right location, she pressed the tip of the blade just below the edge of the bandage. "And here, I think. Correct, Eric?"

Eric smelled the faint sweet scent of jasmine spiced with ginger. Her own creation, he remembered. After all that had happened since they'd last met—to themselves, to the world— she remained the same. It was as if the events in the world didn't affect her directly. She was beyond their touch, as she'd been beyond his bullets.

"Well, Eric?" Angel twisted the blade, adding pressure. A drop of blood spurted onto the shiny metal. "Am I correct? Would you not say those were the locations where you shot me?"

"Approximately," Eric said.

She laughed, the small white teeth glistening like buttered corn. "Then I should be dead, no? Instant kill, *n'est-ce pas?*"

"That's what I thought."

The steel ball bearings shifted in their sockets. "You mean, you *hoped.*" She twisted the knife harder, gouging the flesh. Eric didn't flinch. "Poor, Eric. Forced to make love to me the whole night, just so he could get past my guards and close enough to kill me."

"It was a dirty job," Eric shrugged.

The captain roared with laughter. "Quite a tongue on that boy, Angel my love."

"That will be the first to go," she smiled. "But not the last." She glanced at his crotch, showed more teeth. "When I am through, poor Eric will be minus many things. Including his little friend here."

"Now, now, Angel," the man cautioned. "I promised you Ravensmith, but not the girl. That's business. Look at that figure, that face. I'd wager whoever buys her will keep her tied on her back with her legs spread apart for a week at least."

Angel glanced at Tracy for the first time since entering the room. She didn't like what she saw. "I don't care what you do with her."

"Hmmm. Perhaps a few sessions with the crew will break her in properly." He smiled at Tracy. "Though I warn you, young lady, the women will be even rougher with you than the men. Depraved lot, eh, Griffin?"

Griffin nodded. "We try, Captain."

Angel ignored the patter, her eyes locked on Eric's. "You still haven't guessed it, have you? How I survived."

"You used a double, I suppose. A sister, a cousin. Somebody you hired for just such possibilities." He shrugged. "It doesn't matter."

"It doesn't *matter?*" She pulled the knife away from his oozing wound. With her free hand she reached up and unzipped the sailing jacket she wore over her jeans. She was naked underneath.

"My, my," the captain grinned with mock surprise.

Her breasts were large for an oriental's, but firm and perfectly round. Her long dark nipples budded straight out like thorns. Between her breasts, slightly to the left and over the heart, was a small round scar no larger than a mole. Another was located a few inches lower. "No double," she hissed. "Me! You shot me."

Eric was confused. The scars were right where he'd shot her all right, but they weren't large enough to be bullet wounds. Besides, if he'd actually shot her there, she'd be dead. Unless . . .

"Ahhh," she nodded, pleased at Eric's expression. "Sweet Eric sees now."

Eric sighed. "Fallows."

"Yes, Dirk was kind enough to come to my aid. Providing me with your description and a bulletproof vest to conceal under my coat. He was under orders to have me killed, but he had a plan. He always had a plan. Of course he could do no less, considering he was my business partner of several years." She zipped her jacket closed. "However, I wish he would have warned me how much it would hurt, even with the special apparel."

"Fallows likes surprises," Eric said.

"It was hard to understand what he liked. He made me swear not to kill you, though that was my first desire. But one discovers quickly that it is best never to go against Dirk's wishes. He could be most ruthless." She smirked lewdly. "Especially in bed. Much more selfish than you in that area, Eric. *Tu te souviens de moi?*" Do you remember?

"Seulement dans mes cauchemars." Only in my nightmares.

She raised the knife in a stabbing stance, but the captain grabbed her wrist with surprising agility for someone of his considerable bulk.

"Not yet, Angel. We still haven't discussed the map with your friend."

She tried to twist free, but his grip was iron. The blood drained from her hand. "He knows nothing about the map. I know him. He would have nothing to do with Alabaster or his map."

"Perhaps. But we can't be certain that this isn't just a stall while Alabaster makes a deal with someone else." He released her wrist, his finger imprints still glowing on her skin. "After all, Mr. Ravensmith has a reputation, even out here on the wide open sea. You know what they call you, Mr. Ravensmith?"

Eric shook his head.

"The Warlord. Quaint, eh?"

"Surprising."

"Not at all. You were the Warlord of a group a few months ago. And of course what you and your friends did to Savvytown is the stuff legends are made of. And the primitive souls still alive in California need legends, my friend. They need heroes and villains."

"I guess we know which role you've chosen?" Tracy said.

"Indeed," the captain nodded. "The one that pays better."

"But not without cost." She stared at his twisted features.

"This little ol' thing?" he asked, pointing at his face. "A misunderstanding. Told my barber a little around the edges. His hand slipped." He roared with laughter. Griffin chuckled next to him.

"The Long Beach Halo," Angel explained.

The captain looked up, no longer smiling. His moist black eye glared from under the cliff of gnarled flesh. "A slight miscalculation. Back when it all started, after the quakes, some business associates and I stole a ship and tried to go through that damned Halo, get back to civilization. Most aboard were killed by the Halo, others were killed by the navy gunboats waiting outside, warning us to turn back. We made a run for it, but they forced us back with gunfire. Three of us survived, myself, the captain, and his son. Until the water and food ran low. I waited until they were asleep, then . . ." He made a slashing gesture across his neck. "And then there was one."

"A new captain."

"The wheel keeps spinning, my friend. Besides, they looked even worse than I did." Suddenly he became animated, excited. "My crew even has a nickname for me. This is great, you'll love it. Guess what they call me? Guess."

No one spoke.

"Rhino." He beamed with pride. "Classic, right? Captain Rhino. Like something Robert Louis Stevenson would write. Christ, I love it."

"Children," Angel muttered disgustedly.

The thunder of running feet sounded outside the stateroom. A woman's gaunt face leaned through the doorway. She had a ring through one nostril and a ring through one ear lobe. A thin silver chain connected them. Teeth dangled from the chain, some of them human. "Captain!"

"Yes, Crow?"

"Spotted another ship ahead."

Rhino's interest perked up. "What kind?"

"Looks like a Valiant 47."

"Come on, woman. Give me the stats."

"Well, she can't hold a candle to *The Centurion* here, but she's a beauty. One-piece fiberglass hull with high-density foam floors and stringers. Got a stainless steel tie-rod which anchors the cabin roof to the external lead keel. Teak and ash woodwork."

"Status?"

"Dead in the water. Half a dozen men and a

couple women on deck waving at us for help. Looks like the mast split or something."

Rhino smiled, half of his mouth curling up, the other half frozen in a swamp of scar tissue. "Well, then, let's get on with what we do best, eh."

"And the passengers?" Crow asked, nodding her head. It made the teeth on her chain clack like dice.

He waved a bored hand. "The usual. Save the women. Kill the men on sight." He started out of the cabin, shoving Crow ahead of him. "Battle stations, everyone."

"What about them?" Angel asked, pointing at Eric and Tracy.

Rhino hesitated, considering. He plucked at the rubber band around his wrist, stretched it out, and let it snap against his skin. "I tend to think you're right. They don't know anything about Alabaster or any fucking map. And we didn't find anything in the canoe. Still, first things first. We take care of the little darling waiting up ahead, then you can kill your old chum. But the girl we sell with the others we're about to pick up. Griffin, post someone outside the cabin. Anything pokes out of the door, kill it." He marched off, cheerfully alive with the demands of command.

Angel slammed the door shut behind them. The lock clicked into place.

Tracy ran to the porthole, pressing her face against the glass as they raced toward the disabled ship. She could see the people aboard waving for help, looking happy now that someone was coming.

"Christ, Eric, they'll slaughter them."

"Probably."

"What can we do?"

Eric shook his head. "Watch."

They stared out the porthole. The people on the ship waved and cheered as they sped closer.

8.

Rhino smiled, showing large dark teeth behind his scarred lips. "Everyone armed?"

"Armed and stationed, Cap," Griffin said.

"Then let's party." He rubbed his hands together energetically. "And keep the more gaudy members of the crew toward the stern. We don't want to scare our new friends. Just yet."

"Already done. Devon and Rilke are stashed behind the dinghies. And after seeing what that Ravensmith guy and his chick did to their cousins last night, the Peterson brothers have scrubbed that makeup shit off their faces. Fresh as choirboys, Cap, 'cept for their natural ugly, which they can't much help."

Rhino nodded, looked around the deck. "Where's Crow?"

"Guarding the prisoners. She's pissed about it though. Wants in on the real action."

"She what?" Rhino asked, stretching his rubber band.

Griffin instantly realized he'd said something wrong. His voice went quiet. "Said she wanted in on the action."

"The action, huh? Well, shit, tell her maybe later we'll vote her fucking Prom Queen."

Griffin didn't say anything.

Rhino spun angrily, his lumpy face glowering six inches above Griffin's. "Tell her she'll do what the fuck she's told, just like everybody else on this pissbucket." He stopped, panting the minty scent of toothpaste into Griffin's face. Suddenly he snapped the rubber band on his wrist. When he spoke again, his voice was calmer, though it practically vibrated with pressure. He exaggerated each whispered syllable. "Are the weapons out of sight?"

"Y-Yes, Captain." Griffin's foot nudged the crossbow he'd commandeered from Eric's salvaged canoe. One of the perks of his rank. The bow lay in the shadows at his feet, already cocked and loaded with the same bolt they'd yanked out of Johnny Peterson's chest. Extra bolts stuck out of the top of Griffin's suede boots like a feather bouquet.

The other crew members standing around the deck also had their weapons hidden, but within easy reach. Out of the corners of their eyes they watched Rhino, waiting for his signal to use them.

Angel stood next to Rhino, her arms crossed, not bothering to hold on to anything despite the bumpy ride. The sea breeze fluffed and tossed her glossy black hair, but she didn't notice. Her eyes were fixed on their nearing target.

"Any orders, Cap?" Griffin asked.

Rhino clamped his hand on Griffin's shoulder. Despite his huge bulk, he had small delicate hands, so smooth and slender they might have once been used on hand cream commercials. Though the fingers were fragile looking, they commanded all the enormous strength of his two hundred sixty-eight pounds. He squeezed Griffin's shoulder until the shorter man winced with pain, feeling the bones shift slightly, grinding like twigs. It was a childish display of power, Rhino realized, but just the kind that most impressed these oafs. No matter how brilliant his strategies had proven over the past few months, no matter how much profit he had brought them, they still reacted with more awe to a silly demonstration of brute strength and physical cruelty. They suspected anyone with more brains than brawn was basically weak. Only Angel knew better.

Griffin's knees sagged slightly under Rhino's punishing grip. Pound for pound, Griffin was easily the more muscular of the two, a ruthless fighter who had killed men twice his size. A crewman who had once insulted his ponytail disappeared from the ship that very night. A woman crew member had refused his sexual advances; the next morning her corpse was found dragging behind the ship, only the torso and head hadn't yet been eaten by sharks. No one aboard messed with Griffin again.

Except Rhino. Stuffed inside that ageless,

shapeless lump of a body was a power and energy that frightened them all.

"Good job, my friend," Rhino said, releasing Griffin's shoulder and slapping him happily on the back. "Nothing to do now but wave and smile. Wave and smile." He grinned, slipping one thick arm around Angel's shoulder and lifting his other in a friendly wave to the ship's passengers.

Griffin tried to raise his left hand, but the shoulder was too numb from Rhino's grip. He lifted his right instead and waved. The rest of the crew also waved.

Angel stood impassive, frowning, wearing Rhino's heavy arm like a Siberian shawl. She did not smile; she did not wave. She watched.

The passengers from the disabled ship waved back, cheered, hugged each other with relief.

Rhino's grin broadened on the good half of his face. He waved animatedly now, like someone's rube uncle in a home movie. "Come on in." He chuckled, straightening his jacket over the bulging .38 S&W tucked into his waistband. "The water's just fine."

They sailed closer. The orange sky reflecting off Rhino's dead scars made his face look on fire. He stepped behind the searchlight, letting the cool shadow quench his face. And hide it from the strangers.

When they were close enough to hear, Rhino cupped his hands to his mouth and shouted to the stranded passengers. "Ahoy there. Someone call for a tow truck."

"Thank God," a woman shouted back, tears streaming from her eyes. "Thank God."

"Well, get your AAA cards ready, folks. We'll be there in a few minutes. Mastercard and Visa welcomed."

The passengers laughed happily.

So did Rhino.

"God, look at them. They think he's their savior." Tracy backed away from the porthole and turned away. "I don't want to see what happens next."

Eric was gathering up the girlie magazines from the bunks. "You want to give me a hand."

"Christ, Eric. This is no time for sex magazines."

He was on his knees, dragging his arm under one of the bunks. His hand swept out some dirty underwear, a rolled up sweat sock, a copy of *Penthouse* that had been torn in half.

"Maybe you're right," she sighed, collapsing on one of the bunks. She lazily picked at a magazine next to her called *Blue Boy*. All naked men. "We could screw during the whole attack," she said bitterly. "Then we won't notice what's happening."

Eric moved quickly around the cabin, stacking the magazines.

Tracy watched him a minute. "Did you notice?"

"Notice what?"

"Your friend, uh, Angel."

"Her real name is Phan. Suzette Phan. Her father was a high official in the Diem government, her mother the wife of a French diplomat."

"Whatever. Did you notice what she was wearing?"

"Not much."

"I mean her jeans. The brand."

Eric tossed *Blue Boy* on the pile and looked at Tracy. "The brand of her jeans?"

"Yeah, they were Lee's. Same as mine."

"So?"

Tracy shrugged. "So nothing. Just an observation, that's all. Even in hopeless situations like this you notice the dumbest things. Suddenly I'm fashion conscious. First Goldie Hawn, now Gloria Vanderbilt." She pounded her fist into the wall with frustration. She wouldn't let him see any tears, never again. *"Shit!"*

Eric glanced out the porthole, watched the helpless ship get closer and closer. Above them they heard Rhino bellow out a greeting, joking with the passengers as they hugged each other and thanked him. Within minutes they would be there. Then the carnage.

He looked past the ship now, trying to get a fix on their location. There wasn't much to see out there anymore. The ocean water was splashed with an orange sheen from the Long Beach Halo. A quarter of a mile to the left a dozen tops of buildings stuck out of the water like half-submerged milk cartons. Some of them

74

had as much as five or six stories showing, others just barely one. "We're in downtown Los Angeles, near Third and Grand."

"How do you know?"

"That's the Crocker Bank Building. Used to be fifty-four stories tall. Now it's about four."

She stood up enough to peek through the porthole, then flopped back down again shaking her head. "Jesus."

Eric stared out at the important office buildings once occupied by members of the *Fortune* 500. They looked decapitated, little boxes made of stone and steel and glass, floating on an orange ocean.

"It looks like a toilet bowl out there," Tracy said.

He smiled, sat next to Tracy on the bunk. "In 'Nam I knew a man pinned down in a foxhole, laid on the stinking corpses of his buddies for almost thirty-six hours before figuring it was safe enough to crawl away. Later he told me all he thought about the whole time he was lying there, smelling the stench of their rotting bodies, was where he might have torn his high school-letter sweater one night three years before. Kept playing back that whole evening over and over while lying there with his face pressed against the bleeding guts of his sergeant, retracing his steps, mentally searching everyplace he'd been that night for a nail or something that might have ripped his sweater."

"Spooky. Did he figure it out?"

"Yeah. He remembered a piece of metal trim

that was bent back on the door of his girl friend's Buick. Snagged it after a marathon necking session when she dropped him off at home. Pictured the car perfectly. The Gumby doll hanging from the mirror, the empty 7up bottle on the floor, the Cliff Notes for *Scarlet Letter* wedged in the back seat. Only trouble was, he couldn't remember what sport he'd played to win that letter. Or the name of his school. Not even the name of his girl friend."

"And the moral is?"

"What moral?"

She gave him a look and nodded. "Right. I'll be okay."

Overhead they heard the pounding of footsteps running for position.

Tracy popped up, pressed her face to the porthole, waving desperately at the passengers. They didn't notice her. She started to unfasten the porthole. "Maybe they can hear me now."

Eric reached over her shoulder and slammed the porthole shut.

"What are you doing?" she demanded, trying to pull his hand away. "We can warn them!"

"Not without Rhino and Angel hearing you. They'll be down here in half a minute performing open heart surgery on us."

"But all those people, Eric. We've got to try."

"Right now those people are my only hope for escape."

"Again with escape. You haven't forgotten we're not alone, have you? That this whole damned ship is crawling with armed maniacs?"

"That's why that ship out there is so important. Everyone topside will be occupied with them. That leaves only the guard they posted outside for me to deal with."

Tracy backed away from him, her face pinched with emotion. "God, Eric. Sometimes I forget."

"Forget what?"

"Forget how cold and ruthless you can be. I mean I know all about your past, your hitch in 'Nam with that group of assassins. And all that Indian crap you learned from the Hopis when you were a kid. But this." She shook her head, took a deep breath. "You're willing to use the slaughter of all those people as a *diversion* for your escape?"

"Yes," he said, returning to the pile of magazines he'd stacked.

Tracy followed him. "What do you think the world will think about us? I mean if we ever get out of here, back to the mainland. You were a history professor, what will history say about what we've done?"

"They'll say we acted like savages, selfishly and with little regard for human life other than our own. And they'll be right." He fixed his sharp reddish-brown eyes on her. "But as long as Timmy's alive, I don't care what they think or say. Besides, it's the survivors who write history, so in the end they'll think what we tell them."

She looked out the porthole, read the name of the ship. *Home Run.* The passengers were leaning over the rails, reaching out. She could see the smiles on their faces. She wondered briefly if any of them were wearing Lee jeans.

Behind them the tops of the office buildings peeked out of the flat ocean like gravestones. Here lies Los Angeles, AKA Tinseltown, The Big Orange, Sin City, Cocaine Gulch. Rest In Soggy Peace.

"I'm going with you," she said quietly.

"I thought you didn't like the odds."

"They've improved. Besides, I don't think I want to stay to see the show." She shrugged. She wanted to add oh yeah, I happen to love you more than my own life. To say that she hadn't really wanted to stay behind here without him before, but had made the grand gesture, knowing he'd have a better chance without her. But she didn't say any of that because he'd just stare at her embarrassed, with the memory of Annie knotting his tongue.

She clapped her hands together enthusiastically. "Well, I made my big humanity speech, now let's get the hell off this zoo."

"Okay, give me a hand with these magazines."

"Those? What for?"

"They're going to get us out of here."

Rhino had two memories of childhood, both of them bad.

First, his name. His real name, that is.

John Smith.

Not even a middle initial, for Christ's sake. Just John Smith, as if his parents had used up

78

all their creativity coming up with John.

"It's bad enough we're stuck with the last name of Smith," he once complained to his parents over morning Rice Krispies. "But couldn't you have been a little more imaginative with my first name?"

His father, James Smith, had looked confused as he sliced a banana into his cereal. "I don't understand."

"He doesn't like his name," his mother, Jane Smith explained.

"He doesn't like John? What's wrong with John? Strong tradition, John is. John Hancock, John Milton, John Kennedy, John Updike, John, uh, uh . . ."

"John Wayne," Jane Smith added. "Johnny Carson, John Travolta, Elton John. The list goes on and on."

Fearing that his parents would too, young John Smith just shook his head, pushed the soggy cereal away, and took the shortcut back to school for football practice. He was team manager. Which meant he got to haul water when the players were thirsty and toss towels to them when they trotted dripping out of the shower. He didn't mind. It gave him access to the lockers while the others were out on the field grunting their guts out. During his three years of junior high and three years of high school, team manager had translated into a lot of emptied wallets and missing watches. Locks were changed twice during his tenure there, but he'd never been caught.

He had been a big boy even then, with a thick body that had no particular shape. It wasn't fat exactly, but neither was it muscular. No clothes seemed to fit right. It was a misshapen blob of flesh, formless like his name.

For a couple years the coach pleaded with John to try out for the team, but he always refused. He could see no profit in banging heads and eating dirt. Not compared with what riches awaited him in the silent lockers.

At first, the members of the team had teased him, calling him Fatty, Blimp Boy, and such. It didn't bother him much; at least it was better than John Smith. But once, after a particularly bad practice in which the coach had really chewed their asses off, they'd come back cranky and surly and ganged up on John, trying to force him into the shower with his clothes on.

John Smith had not wanted to go.

Before the coach finally came in to investigate the ruckus, John had broken the quarterback's thumb, twisted the halfback's ankle, cracked the center's ribs, and bruised a tackle's eye. The worst thing that had happened to John had been a torn pocket on his shirt, which his mother sewed that night during *The Fugitive*.

Breaking the thumb had been the most fun. He'd straddled Tom Jenkins' chest, pinning his arms to the concrete floor. Then, while fighting the others off, he'd yanked back on Tom's thumb so hard the web of skin between the thumb and index finger tore. Bone ground against bone like squealing brakes until the thumb snapped. Tom's scream bounced eerily around the shower stalls.

John had not been punished by the school. After all, he had only been defending himself. Nor did the team members try to gain revenge. The coach's only reaction was again to encourage John to try out for the team.

But John had learned a valuable lesson. About himself and others. He learned that he was not afraid to administer pain to someone else if necessary. He realized that he could just as easily have snapped Tom Jenkins' neck as thumb. It didn't matter. *He felt no guilt.*

And he learned that public displays of power go a long way toward controlling others. Before the incident, although he'd been ranked third in his class academically, no one had paid any attention to him. But after word got around school of what had happened in the showers, no one called him any names again. Younger boys talked to him with respect and awe. Older guys nodded hello. Girls giggled and whispered, but with curiosity.

The second childhood memory was about sex.

His first time.

It was after a football game. They were celebrating their 27–14 victory over arch-rival University High. The party, as usual, boasted a couple kegs of beer that some of last year's grads brought, and some joints supplied by Dennis Bedlow, proud holder of the worst attendance record in the school.

The party was at Valerie Rhinehart's house because her parents were at a fat farm for the weekend. Valerie, the head cheerleader, had been dumped last week by Tom Jenkins after going steady for two years. She got drunk almost immediately, threw up on Tom's date, and passed out in the bathroom. A couple guys carried her up to her bedroom, discussed jumping her, but chickened out. That's when John went up.

He had never had any kind of sex, except masturbation, and he hadn't much enjoyed that. Dating had never really interested him. The idea of spending money on someone you didn't know very much seemed stupid. Where's the profit, the payoff? It had to be more than just ejaculating. He could do that by himself and it didn't cost anything. If there was something special, he wanted to know about it.

Valerie was still in her cheerleader outfit, the short skirt folded up revealing long athletic legs. One of the guys had jokingly placed her Snoopy doll face down between her legs. John plucked it away, tossing it onto the floor.

What if she wakes up? he wondered, and a strange thought bloomed in his mind: *I'll kill her.* As simple as that. No malice or hate or fear or desire. Just a fact.

It didn't take him long to work her cheerleading panties down her legs, though he had some trouble unhooking them from her ankles. Valerie shifted once, but her eyes remained closed, a slight snore puffing her lips.

He dropped his pants to his knees and climbed onto the bed. No point in getting undressed himself. This shouldn't take long.

He poked his finger into her vagina, which was warm and wet. Sticky, he thought, like spilled Coke. He grabbed his penis, which was semistiff, and plunged it into her.

He pumped against her for several minutes, stopping once to rearrange her legs because her knees were starting to chafe against his wide hips. He continued pumping for several more minutes, but nothing happened. He started to pull out.

Valerie's eyes opened.

Concerned that she might scream, his hand reached for a pillow. Smother her, I guess, he thought, surprised at his own calmness.

"Don't stop," she whispered, licking his ear.

He dropped the pillow and continued moving against her. She panted in his ear, which annoyed him. He liked her better unconscious. Finally he felt the semen boiling through his penis and shooting into her.

"Yes, yes," she gasped. "I want it in me. All of it."

He wanted to giggle. Such a corny line. The trash she must be reading.

He got up quickly and pulled up his pants.

"Don't go," she slurred drunkenly. But when she jumped up to stop him, she swooned and dropped to her knees. She barfed on the

Snoopy doll.

John left her kneeling next to her bed like someone in prayer.

He'd learned another valuable lesson that would guide him through his later life. *He didn't like sex*. It had no effect on him. He tried it again a few times at intervals of a couple years, but to his relief, it never got any better. The realization was thrilling, as exhilarating as rolling in snow. It made him invulnerable to women. And it gave him plenty of time to pursue other interests, namely money.

Those interests eventually led him to the presidency of DataStat, an information warehouse that other computers were able to tap into, for a fee. In the course of his rise to power, he had several times found it necessary to impose the lessons he'd learned as a child. Two competitors were killed at his request to allow a profitable merger. An argumentative lawyer lectured to him about ethics in front of his vice-presidents and in midsentence received a bottle of Perrier across his cheek in reply. The surgical restructuring of the face was paid for by the company as was the partial disability for eighty percent loss of sight in one eye. It was reported as an industrial accident. No one ever questioned his ethics again. Aloud.

As the years passed, his millions of dollars hadn't changed his attitude about his name or about sex.

But since his adventures in the Long Beach

Halo, he had changed. Not just in his hideous face, which he almost enjoyed now, as if it were a mask behind which he could retreat. But other things had changed, in his body. He couldn't sleep. One or two hours a night was all he could manage, and sometimes not even that. It was not uncommon for him to stay awake for three or four days at a time. He didn't feel especially tired—in fact, just the opposite. He was bursting with excess energy, always restless, always on the move. It had made him impatient, quick to sudden flares of temper. He felt like a nuclear reactor on the verge of a meltdown.

Angel had suggested the rubber band around the wrist. An old home remedy to help people quit smoking. Whenever they craved cigarettes, they would snap the rubber bands against their wrists. Aversion therapy. That's what Rhino did when he felt his rage boiling at the back of his brain, flames crackling behind his eyeballs. Sometimes it worked and he would be in control again.

And sometimes it didn't work.

"Too bad I didn't know you earlier, my Angel," Rhino said. "Before this city was turned into a giant aquarium. It would've been a kick showing you around. Behind that building over there"—he pointed with his short delicate finger—"is the Original Pantry. Great restaurant. Bunch of guys in white shirts and bow ties acting like waiting on tables is something they do to relax between cashing dividend checks. Served the best breakfast in L.A."

"I don't eat breakfast," Angel replied simply.

"Right, right. No breakfast. Small lunch. Tea for dinner. Christ, who was your nutritionist? Gandhi?"

She glanced over at his lumpy, shapeless body, then up into his face. She arched a thin crescent eyebrow, saying nothing.

Rhino laughed. "Beautiful. Beautiful expression, like in one of those old film *noir* movies. Joan Crawford blowing cigarette smoke up Bette Davis' nose. You must practice that." He stretched the rubber band around his wrist, but didn't release it. "What a pair we make, Angel. Dragon Lady and the Phantom of the Opera. My, my."

He chattered on energetically, but his eyes remained fixed on the approaching ship. He could feel the energy building in his body, buzzing along his raw nerves like exposed high voltage wires. He was afraid to look at his hands, thinking that if he did he might see the nerve endings boring out through the skin like hungry worms. Last night he'd had only forty minutes of sleep, the night before barely an hour. But he was practically vibrating with energy now. Even the scar tissue on his face tingled as *The Centurion* swept closer to the stranded *Home Run*.

"Toss us a line," a young man from the ship shouted. Rhino thought he looked like a famous tennis player, one of the Swedish ones with a name like smelly cheese, but he couldn't be sure since he had always hated tennis. Bratty kids with sour faces and no personalities. Not like the sports heroes of his time. Mantle, Namath, Chamberlain.

"Toss them a line, Devon," Rhino said.

Devon hoisted the rope next to him, one end of which was secured to a cleat. He tossed it over the side to the *Home Run*, less than fifteen feet away now. The rope seemed to hover over the water for a moment, uncoiling, before bouncing onto the other ship's deck. The blond boy waved thanks. Devon just stared and waited for the signal, his right hand flexing toward his hidden bow.

Rhino counted people on the *Home Run*. Five men and three women. All apparently unarmed. They didn't look dehydrated or scrawny, either. Probably a good supply of food and water aboard. Who knows what else? But even if there wasn't, the women alone would be enough. One was close to forty, but still looked pretty fit. The other two were mid-twenties. No raving beauties, but nice bodies worth something at Liar's Cove.

He unfastened the top brass button of his jacket. When he unbuttoned the other two, it would signal the crew to attack, first with a wave of arrows, then hand to hand if necessary.

The use of guns was strictly last resort. Ammunition was too precious and rare. Besides they would probably need it for the trip to Liar's Cove, not to mention while they were there.

A few more ropes were exchanged between ships, with crew members from both sides pulling their crafts closer to the other. The *Home Run* rode lower in the water, which pleased Rhino since it would mean easier access for his crew.

He unfastened another button.

The hulls of the two ships bumped. Ropes were tied off to secure the ships.

The older woman leaned over the rail and waved up at Rhino and Angel. She didn't seem to wince at the sight of Rhino's mangled face. "Thank you so much," she said. "We've been stranded out here for almost two days. The rig's split and we didn't want to risk snapping it off altogether. We thought the current might take us closer to land." She shrugged, embarrassed. "But I'm afraid none of us are really sailors. It's my husband's yacht, but he died." Her voice trailed off in what seemed like a sad memory. "Anyway, thanks again."

"Our pleasure." Rhino touched two fingers to the brim of his cap in a snappy salute. "Code of the sea demands that we help. Right, Angel?"

Angel spoke softly, but with an edge. "Have you any more people below deck? I mean wounded who might require medical assistance."

"Do you have a doctor aboard?"

"No," Angel replied. "But we have a trained army nurse." She nodded toward the bow of the ship where Kelly Furst stood. Kelly was black, her hair swirling in a springy tangle, of dreadlocks. Her short khaki pants had been torn off high at the thigh to reveal long shapely legs, thick with muscles. The tight, green army T-shirt hugged her wiry rugged upper body.

As they spoke, Angel noticed the crew members of the *Home Run* drifting back from the rails, almost in unison. She spun toward Rhino, whose nimble fingers were nudging at his final button. "Wait, something's wrong here."

But too late. The button popped free and the crew of *The Centurion* grabbed for their weapons.

Crow leaned against the wall and listened to the stomping feet overhead, the twanging of bows, the thudding of arrows as they split wood and cleaved ribs, the occasional scream of pain as something sharp sliced through skin and organs.

God, she wished she were up there now.

She had a good mind to bust down that fucking door and skewer those two right now. The Warlord, huh? She'd heard about him here and there. A woman she'd slept with in Liar's Cove had been at Savvytown when Ravensmith had rolled through there, kicking the shit out of the bunch that ran that rat hole. Claimed that he saved her life and a lot of others. She grinned, sliding her arrow onto her bow. She'd like to see him try something now. At least that would give her a couple more teeth to add to her collection.

She touched a finger to the gold chain that ran from her nose to her ear lobe, flicked the teeth that dangled there. They clicked together like an abacus. One from each animal or person she'd killed since the quakes. Getting them out of the dead body was often the hardest part. She carried pliers in her belt for just that reason, though once she had to smash a guy's jaw with a hammer, then dig the tooth out with a knife. He'd given up his life easier than that damn tooth.

Something heavy thumped on deck above her. She recognized the sound of a dead body. She looked at her watch. Seemed to be taking them longer than usual to finish this bunch off. Maybe she could sneak up, just for a minute, just long enough to fire off one lousy arrow.

No. Better not. If Rhino saw her, or that Angel bitch . . . Well, it was better not to remember what she'd seen them do before to someone who'd disobeyed an order.

"'Everyday, it's a-gettin' closer,'" she sang softly. "'Goin' faster than a roller coaster . . .'" It was the Buddy Holly song they'd played Prom Night fifteen years ago, when she was elected Prom Queen. She'd never forget that night. The theme had been Those Fabulous 'Fifties and the boys had all greased their hair and combed it into duck tails. She'd been in charge of hiring the band, The Judas Goats, though they'd changed their names to Daryl and the Do Wops for that one night.

Then the announcement of Prom Queen. She'd been so sure Karen Hale would get it. . . .

Two shots exploded. Jesus, even Rhino was getting into this one. That was unusual, he didn't usually like to use any bullets. Maybe she should check it out, see if they needed a hand? Better wait a couple more minutes.

She'd made the mistake of telling Rhino about Prom Night once. Now he made fun of her all the time. That and the fact that her father was a dentist.

The stateroom door smashed open in front of her, splinters darting around her like porcupine needles. She saw Eric diving into the narrow passageway, something thick in his hands. She didn't bother determining what it was. She hoisted the Jennings compound hunting bow, the arrow's Bjorn nock already clipped to the string. Quickly she drew the eighty pounds of pressure, leveled the arrow on the largest part of Eric's body, his chest, and released her three fingers from the string. Though only ten feet separated Crow and Eric, the arrow launched out of the bow at two hundred feet per second.

"This will never work," Tracy frowned.
"Sure it will."
"You'll get us killed."

91

"Want to bet?"

She finished tying her knot around one stack and looked up at him. "What if you're wrong?"

"Then you win the bet." He tossed her a couple more magazines. "I don't need these."

Using the prong from her belt, Tracy pried the staples out of the spines of each magazine, but otherwise left them intact. Her right thumbnail was torn and bleeding from pulling on stubborn staples. She bit the jagged piece of nail off, spitting it onto the floor. "You owe me a manicure, buster."

"Tonight," he said.

Eric tore another strip of cloth from the filthy sheet he'd taken from one of the bunks. He knotted it in place to the stack he'd been working on. "All done," he announced. "Let's do it."

"Suddenly I wish we'd decided to make love instead."

"Tonight. After the manicure."

"Before."

"Before *and* after. Okay?"

She took a deep breath, lifted her stack of stapleless magazines. "Right."

Eric had two stacks of magazines, both thicker than Tracy's, both with their staples still intact. Each was bound as tightly as possible with two parallel strips of linen that compressed the pages until they were hard as steel. Each strip had a loop tied at it. Eric slid each arm through a loop and grasped the other with his hands. He stood there with the solid stacks of skin magazines strapped to each arm like two small shields.

"I don't know, Eric," Tracy said, shaking her head. "I still think you'd be better off with a hunk of wood or something."

"There isn't enough wood in the room, nor enough time to get to it. And what little that's here is too thin, even stacked. Paper actually absorbs the shock better. It'll be like trying to shoot through the Manhattan phone book."

"In theory, damn it. *Theory.*"

Eric pressed his ear to the door.

He heard Crow singing to herself. "'Everyday, it's a gettin' closer . . .'"

Softly he ran his fingers along the edge of the door looking for the right spot. When he found it, he stepped back, measuring the distance with his leg. "Ready?"

Tracy's voice was raspy, hollow. "Ready."

"You've got to move right away, Trace. Before she gets a second shot off."

"It's the first one I'm worried about."

"That makes two of us," he said and snapped his foot into the door just above the lock. It sprang open in a shower of shattered wood and he dove through.

It reminded Eric of one of those 3-D movies where things are always flying out into the audience. Only this arrow was real. And it was flying right at him.

He'd bashed through the door and immediately curled into a tuck-and-roll position, making the smallest possible target. After all, his "shields" weren't very large, and he'd only have one chance. He hoped Tracy was ready, because there was no way he'd be able to block a second shot. Maybe not even the first.

He bumped up against the wall, felt his chest wounds tearing open under the bandages. Suddenly the magazines seemed heavy as iron, much too heavy to lift. How could he ever have thought this would work?

But somehow he wrestled them up in front of his chest just as Crow's aluminum shaft slapped into the glossy pages, burrowing through *Penthouse*, two *Playboys*, *Beaver*, *Club*, and three *Hustlers*, barely poking through the left breast of the cover girl for *Platinum* before stopping with a *Penthouse* and *Swank* to spare.

Crow didn't pause. She pulled another arrow from her hip quiver, nocked it into the string, and began the smooth draw, the palm of her hand anchoring at her chin as she took aim.

Tracy jumped screaming and whooping through the doorway like a Hollywood Indian, the three stapleless magazines raised over her head. She flung them at Crow like Moses hurling the Ten Commandments and quickly stepped back into the stateroom. The magazines burst apart in midair, each page fluttering in a confetti cloud of naked bodies.

Crow released her arrow, but by now her line of vision was so impaired, the arrow zipped off down the passageway and into the galley wall.

She was reaching for another arrow when she felt Eric's hands closing around her throat.

Eric yanked her off her feet, tossing her over his hip. The corridor was too narrow for proper leverage, and her head and feet banged into the wall on the way down to the floor. But she punched and clawed at him all the way down.

He felt as if a rabid rat were gnawing through his chest where he'd been wounded, but he hung onto her throat, digging his thumbs into her windpipe.

Crow brought her right hand down, wriggling it into the small of her back where her knife was sheathed. Her fingertips grazed the handle, closed around it. Awkwardly she eased it out of the leather sheath, mentally picking the spot on his back where she'd plunge it.

"Nope," Eric said, grabbing the thin gold chain strung between her nose and ear with its grizzly dancing teeth, and yanking it hard. She screamed as the chain tore through the skin of the nostril and ear lobe. In that spasm of pain, her hand uncurled from the knife.

Leaning his weight into his thumbs, Eric felt the cartilage give way in her windpipe. In the time it took for Tracy to help him to his feet, Crow choked to death.

"It worked," Tracy said, marveling at the arrow sticking out of the stack of magazines.

"Yeah," Eric said, clutching his chest. "How about that."

They started for the stairs, listening to the sounds of the battle raging overhead.

Eric nocked an arrow into Crow's bow. "Now for the hard part."

His hand reached for the doorknob just as an explosion thundered outside. The ship tilted to the right, slamming Eric into Tracy and both of them into the wall. As they scrambled to their feet, bracing themselves on the rocking walls, they heard the clunking sound of hunks of debris raining on deck. A man's pitiful scream mixed with a loud whooshing sound.

"What's going on?" Tracy asked.

"Only one way to find out," Eric said, pulling open the door.

The man was running straight at them, his sweater lively with flames. The fire leaped from his sweater up his neck and lit his long blond hair like a torch to a hay stack. Wildly he began slapping at the flames with his hands. Then they, too, caught fire. Next his face. Now he was clawing at his eyes, running blindly toward Eric and Tracy.

Eric didn't know whose side the flaming man was on. It didn't matter anymore. He quickly drew back Crow's bowstring and fired the arrow into the man's heart. He flopped to the deck in a smoldering smoking heap.

One of Rhino's men—Eric recognized him as Griffin—ran over, grabbed the fiery corpse by the heels, and dragged him to the edge of the ship, flipping him over the side. A sizzling hush steamed from the ocean when he hit.

Griffin didn't seem to notice Eric and Tracy. After dumping the body, he spun around and leaped onto the *Home Run*, snagging one of its escaping passengers by the collar. Eric saw his own crossbow riding on Griffin's huge muscular back with a rope strap he must have rigged. Eric raised Crow's bow for a shot, but Griffin disappeared amidst the smoke.

The *Home Run*'s deck was a dense jungle of flames. Eric glanced around, trying to figure out what had happened. Most of the passengers from the *Home Run* were in rafts and dinghies, paddling heartily away from their burning ship. A few had not managed to get off in time and were being butchered by the savage crew of *The Centurion*. A leggy black woman and a lanky man were hacking at the ropes binding the two ships together.

Rhino stood at the bow of his ship, leaning over the railing and watching the action aboard the *Home Run*. He didn't look worried, rather somewhat amused. And a little impatient, as if anxious for it all to be over, not because it was dangerous to his ship, but because he was becoming bored and restless.

Less than five feet away from Rhino, a large man had Angel in a crushing full nelson, trying to force her head forward until the neck snapped. Rhino watched without interfering, playing with the rubber band around his wrist. Angel's chin was grinding into her chest and

97

her arms were pinned helplessly. Still Rhino didn't move the three steps to help her.

But then, she didn't need help. Suddenly she snapped her heel back into her attacker's kneecap, loosening but not breaking his grip. She snapped her heel back again. And again. The final time, his kneecap was shattered permanently and it gave way under him. He released his grip on Angel. She rolled out from under him into a front handspring that any gymnast would envy. When she was upright again, she had her balisong knife in hand. She whipped the handles around until the blade reflected the dull orange of the sky. While her attacker struggled to regain his balance, she darted behind him, grabbed a handful of hair, tugged his head backward, and dug her knife into his throat. She dragged the blade in a semicircle across his neck, blood misting her hand.

Rhino shook with laughter and applauded. Eric couldn't hear what he was saying, but whatever it was, Angel ignored him. Then Rhino glanced over his shoulder and met Eric's gaze. He straightened up immediately, pointing his delicate hands in their direction. Angel ran toward them.

"There!" he shouted, dragging his .38 out of his belt and thrusting it in their direction. He squeezed off two shots. The first blew up the door jamb next to Tracy. The second whistled between them, tearing through one of the sails

98

before disappearing out to sea.

"This way," Tracy said, leading Eric to where she'd last seen their canoe. He crouched low and followed her toward the stern. Another shot kicked up a few splinters of deck wood six inches from his left foot. They ducked around a mast.

The canoe lay abandoned, their weapons gone. The backpacks lay open and ravaged, some of their stuff still scattered around for examination.

Two more bullets whizzed by. One pinged off the aluminum railing. The other poked another hole in their canoe's hull.

"You sure this will still float?" Tracy asked as she grabbed one end.

Eric grabbed the other end and they hefted it up. "It'll float. I built air pockets into the bow and stern. It may take on a lot of water, but it'll float. Ready?"

"Yeah."

"One, two." They swung the canoe in a lullaby arc. *"Three!"* With a groan they tossed the canoe over the rail.

"We did it!" Tracy cheered, leaning over the rail. "It's floating."

They heard Angel's footsteps running behind them. They turned, saw the knife clutched in her hand.

A shot cracked through the sound of battle. The bullet pounded into Tracy's hip, shoving her over the rail in a screaming somersault.

Eric spun, his arrow already drawn to his cheek, and fired hastily at Rhino's lumpy body. But Rhino moved faster than Eric thought possible for him, flopping to the deck as the arrow rocketed over his shoulder. Eric didn't wait for another chance. He dropped the bow, grabbed the two paddles, one of the half-filled backpacks, and jumped over the side of the ship.

9.

The orange-tinted ocean flooded through the arrow and bullet holes until the canoe looked like a bowl half filled with tomato soup. Eric kept paddling, gritting his teeth against the jagged pain in his chest. Fresh blood sopped the jersey bandages and dripped like icing down his flat hard stomach, winding along the corrugated muscles.

"What the hell was that all about?" Tracy asked.

Eric dug the paddle into the water, muscled the canoe ahead another few feet. "A setup."

"Yeah, but who was doing the setting?" Tracy was leaning on her left side, her legs stretched out and submerged in the cold water. Her right hand pressed a swath of her jersey sweat shirt against her bloody hip; the left hand bailed water with the Campbell's soup can.

The bullet had chomped through the hip and out the back of her thigh. Eric didn't like the nasty way it was looking, but there was nothing to do about it right now. They had to get to safety first. He could see the pain twisting through her, but she made no complaint. She nibbled her lip and bailed water. After a few minutes of silence, she sighed. "God, I'm tired of being wet."

Eric laughed.

Another explosion drowned his laughter.

They looked back at the two ships, watched a tower of flames spit high into the air along the *Home Run*'s mast. The sails flapped in the breeze like fiery wings.

The Centurion had managed to free itself from the burning ship and was now backing away, its sails puffed with wind. The bow of the ship raged with fire, but Angel was directing several crew members as they battled the flames with buckets of water they hauled up from over the side. Someone was hosing the mainsail with a fire extinguisher, smothering the few flames that licked the edges there.

Two rowboats from the *Home Run* were splashing through the ocean, curving to the left, away from their abandoned ship. Three people sat in one, a single person in the other. Behind them a rubber life raft floated aimlessly with two of their comrades, each sprouting arrows from their backs. The rest of the bodies were unaccounted for.

One of the bodies on the rubber raft hung over the side, with head and arm dangling in the water as if trying to see something down deep.

As Eric and Tracy watched, something tugged at the body once, then again, finally yanking it over the side and under the surface. The water boiled blood to mark the spot, then was calm. The body never reappeared.

Eric and Tracy didn't talk about it. Eric merely paddled the canoe in an arc that swung in the opposite direction.

"Where are they going?" Tracy asked, nodding at the two escaping dinghies.

"Looks like they're heading toward that building."

"Over there," she pointed. "There's a ship waiting behind that Transcontinental Insurance Building." As their canoe slid forward, they could see more of the ship, before hidden by the two protruding stories of the otherwise submerged building. The two surviving rowboats splashed energetically toward the ship, waving a greeting to the crew on board. "You were right, Eric. It was a setup. They wanted to sink *The Centurion*."

"They came damn close. And us with it."

"Wonder why they didn't attack with their ship too?" Tracy asked.

Eric shook his head. "No way. That's a Wellington 63 over there. Nice maxicruiser with NACA air-foil sections and a terrific aft cabin. The high sail area/displacement and sail area/wetted area ratios make it pretty fast. The sail area is nineteen hundred square feet and if it's got any fuel, it's got a two hundred ten horsepower Caterpillar diesel coupled to a variable pitch, three-bladed Hundested prop. But *The Centurion* is a seventy-three-foot staysail schooner with—"

"Stop it!" Tracy hollered and threw a canful of water into Eric's face. She threw the can too, but the string attaching it to the thwart snapped it back before it hit him. The sudden physical effort made Tracy wince with pain, but she kept her eyes boring into Eric's. He stared back, his face dripping with water, his expression merely surprise.

"I'm tired of feeling so goddamned helpless, Eric. Before all this I was an artist, a damn sketch artist for trials, but at least I was respected. I knew my way around the business like a professional." She shifted her hip so she could see him better. "But the kind of things you need to know here, I wasn't prepared for. What plants to eat, how to find drinking water, how to make weapons out of fingernail clippings. Christ, I feel like a baby. And you make it worse."

"Tracy, I didn't—"

"Wait," she interrupted, holding up her hand. "I'm not complaining. Not really. Considering the reality of the kind of world we now live in, that we may live in for the rest of our lives, I'm damned lucky to be with you. But you're damn lucky to be with *me* too, buster. I'm pretty smart, fairly athletic, and a lot sexier than you're likely to find for a long time. It's just that I get a little frustrated sometimes by the way you seem to know so much. How come you always know everything?"

He looked at her and shrugged. "I don't know."

And both burst out laughing at the same time. It was a long laugh that caused as much pain as pleasure. Both clutched their wounds as they shook with laughter. It was a communion of mirth, a lightening of spirits that seemed to even float free of the Long Beach Halo. Eric reached into the water at the bottom of the canoe, gripped Tracy's ankle to steady himself as he laughed. Tracy held onto the gunwales, causing the whole boat to rock precariously. Neither seemed to notice. Afterward, tears brimming in their eyes, smiles still stretching their lips, they fell silent.

Eric stared out over the ocean before him, the long square necks of buildings craning out of the water. Their laughter seemed to still echo across the ocean, perhaps bouncing around inside the buildings, and he thought what a strange sound it was. And how little of it they'd heard since the quakes. How little they'd done.

"You're looking kind of pale, Eric," Tracy said. "How about you doing the bailing and I'll paddle for a while."

"Can you sit up?"

"Sure," she said, but when she tried to curl her legs up, the hip jerked with pain. Her fingers dug into the gunwales until the knuckles glowed white. The jersey cloth fell from her wound and Eric leaned over to inspect.

Jesus, he cursed to himself, but kept an

105

impassive face. The bullet hole had pounded through the hip like a dull nail, charring the flesh around the entry hole. He tore open her pants around the wound. The skin was puckered and the angry red glow of infection was spreading. The bullet had bored straight through and out the back of the thigh, so at least he wouldn't have to dig the slug out.

Eric opened the one half-filled backpack he'd managed to grab before jumping off the ship. A pair of thick socks, two rolls of duct tape, a stick of bee's wax he'd used on his bow string. No medical supplies, no compass, no knife, no food. And with Tracy's wound looking so bad, he'd have to do something quick.

"Reminds me of *The Angry Red Planet*," Tracy said, staring at the wound. "Remember that movie? The giant spider on Mars."

Eric nodded. "We'll paddle over to that building there, rest for the night. Tomorrow we head straight for land."

Tracy looked at him. For Eric to break off his search for Timmy meant that this was serious. "How bad is it? Am I going to lose my leg or what?"

"I don't know."

"Don't pull that crap on me now, Eric. Maybe part of the reason I sometimes feel so frustrated and helpless is that you keep things from me. We're in this together, right?"

"Right," Eric said. "It's too early to tell yet, but I've seen enough bullet wounds to know this one needs immediate attention. We're both too tired to make it to land today. Besides, we'd be idiots to travel during the day anyway. So we hole up in that building until dark and head straight for land, where I have a better chance of treating your leg with herbs and medicinal plants."

Tracy examined her pulpy hip, made a sour face. "What if we don't land near any of the plants you need?"

"Then I find something else."

"What?"

"You really want to know?"

"Yes, damn it."

Eric hesitated. "Maggots."

"Oh Christ, Eric. I'm serious."

"So am I. Maggots ingest dead tissue. A common treatment of infected battle wounds during World War I. We just expose the wound to flies and pretty soon we'll have our maggots."

Tracy swallowed the thickness in her throat. "I've changed my mind about wanting to know everything."

Eric smiled. "Don't worry. I'll have you on your knees paddling this thing in no time."

"Some incentive."

Eric guided the canoe toward the nearest building. Only two and a half stories stuck out of the water, but that would be more than enough. At least a third of the reflective glass plating that encased the building like armor was shattered. Huge gaping holes stared out where floating debris had rammed through. As they neared the building, they could see that the tail of a small Piper plane stuck out of the building. The rest of the plane was lodged in the top floor where it had crashed.

"Rhino and your former playmate are hauling their butts out of here," Tracy said, pointing at *The Centurion*, sails full as it sped away. The *Home Run* still sat quietly in the middle of the ocean, flames engulfing the whole ship, hissing as falling boards touched water. "Did you really sleep with her one night and try to kill her in the morning?"

"Yes. It was the quickest way to get past her guards."

"But she knew who you were all the time."

"Thanks to Fallows. I should've known he'd find a way to turn some profit out of the war." He traced his finger along his scar, the scar that Fallows had given him back in Vietnam.

"Eric, they're coming toward us."

"What?"

"That ship. The one that picked up the passengers. They're sailing right at us."

Eric watched the sails being hauled up, the last of the survivors being pulled aboard, as the ship turned its bow toward them. He could see four or five armed archers standing at the railing, arrows already nocked into the strings.

He dug the paddle into the water, churning at the ocean until the canoe was closing in on the building. His wounded chest throbbed as if the ribs were poking through the skin, tearing at the muscles, but he had no other choice.

"As soon as we land, we search the place for

anything we can turn into weapons."

"Fine, as long as it doesn't involve maggots."

"Check the plane first. See if there's any fuel left. Maybe we can mix a couple Molotov cocktails."

"Okay. But maybe they don't want to harm us. After all, they did try to destroy Rhino and that bunch."

"That doesn't necessarily make them our friends. It could have been a business dispute."

"Business dispute?"

"Look at the flag?"

Tracy shaded her eyes with her hand and peered across the water at the approaching ship. High atop the mast was a fluttering black flag with a skull and crossbones.

"They've got to be kidding," she said. "It's too corny to be real. Pirates?"

Eric backwatered the paddle, easing the canoe up to one of the large holes in the glass. Tracy dragged herself through the hole, cutting her hand on a jagged piece of glass. Eric followed, hopping into the dark dusty room and hauling the canoe in after them.

They turned to face the room they'd entered. A steel filing cabinet stood against the wall, but otherwise the room was empty. The floor was wet and sticky with clumps of seaweed that the ocean washed in every few seconds as another wave lapped through the hole.

Eric anchored the canoe, wedging it behind the filing cabinet. Then he slipped an arm around Tracy's waist and helped her toward the room's only door, which was closed. "We'll find the stairs and climb to the next floor. That'll give us the upper ground advantage. We might even be able to block off the stairs after us."

Tracy reached for the doorknob, turned, and pulled it open.

The three men stood with weapons ready. There was an ax poised over one man's shoulder, another man thrust his makeshift spear against Tracy's stomach, a third man pressed a .22 automatic against Eric's temple. Behind them stood a tall woman with a red bandana tied around her forehead giving orders.

"Kill them now?" the brutish man with the ax asked her hopefully.

Book Two:

ON THE SHIPS

Look now how mortals are blaming the gods, for they say that evils come from us, but in fact they themselves have woes beyond their share because of their own follies.

—Homer

10.

Eric Ravensmith scraped the steel blade against his dry cheek. Though the room was too dark to see anything, he felt the slivers of brown whiskers sprinkled lightly on his chin like tiny leaves. For a moment he thought of himself as a giant sequoia tree, witnessing hundreds of years of human turmoil, but at the end still standing, calm and indifferent in the dark forest. He brushed the whiskers with his hand. He knew without looking that there were dozens of gray ones mixed in with the brown, more than last month. At this rate he'd be all gray by Christmas. He tilted his head back and carefully scraped his neck.

"God, that's an ugly sound," Tracy said. "Like you're munching on a mouthful of beetles. Yech."

Eric smiled, nudging the sharp blade gently over his jugular, decapitating two-day-old whiskers like a hooded headsman.

"Some people, Eric, might think this was a strange time to shave. Not me, you understand, just some people who didn't know you." Her voice echoed in the cold, dark room. "I mean, we've been huddled in this drafty office with the wind whipping off the ocean and nipping at our toes and giving me crow's feet from squinting. We're prisoners again, unarmed again, when you come up with this brilliant way to make a couple knives. So far, so good. But now you sit there *shaving*, for Christ's sake. Do I think that's weird? Hey, no problem."

Eric reached his hand over to where he knew she was lying, grazed her shoulder, then traced the length of her arm until he felt her cold hand. He squeezed it and she squeezed back. Something as invisible as electricity and as thick as blood passed between them in that contact. They just held tight for a few minutes, feeling the building sway and groan with the shifting ocean current.

"How's the hip?"

"We'll have to cut the triple somersault out of our sexual repertoire, but otherwise okay." She coughed, a racking spasm which sent a flare of pain through her hip. "You don't happen to have a couple hungry maggots handy, do you?"

"Hold on, Trace," Eric said, wishing he had something more encouraging to tell her. Hell, he wished he had more to say about a lot of things. He'd never been the shy quiet type, rather a fairly animated conversationalist, able to hold his students' rapt attention semester after semester as he chatted about Da Vinci's financial woes or Napoleon's stomach cancer. But lately with each passing day he seemed to say less and less, reverting to some animal silence that didn't require speech. He didn't like it.

Eric glanced at the door. A stripe of flickering light glowed at the bottom. He heard voices on the other side, but couldn't make out what was said. He didn't have to hear the exact words. He knew that they were the main topic.

Almost immediately upon being captured, Tracy and Eric had been locked back in the same room that they'd crawled into from their canoe. The canoe had been dragged off into another room and they'd been told to wait. On the other side of the building where that Piper had crashed, they had heard the large ship docking. The shouting and arguing of men and women, sounding none too friendly, had been going on since then.

The orange Kool-Aid sky had burned itself out for another and the hazy gray of night took over its watch. That's when Eric saw the Long Beach Halo that enclosed them all as a malevolent guard. Tracy described that phenomenon as a giant Tupperware bowl. "Seals in freshness," she joked, "keeps out ugly refrigerator smells. Not to mention the rest of the world." At first there had been weekly government leaflets dumped from Air Force planes flying over the Halo, describing medical and military efforts underway to rescue the survivors of California, asking for patience. And specifically warning residents not to try to escape by sea through the Halo due to fears of contamination. Every Monday they had come drifting out of the orange haze like a heavenly bulletin from God. But after a while they came every other week. Now monthly. There was still talk of rescue, but not as much of it.

Eric didn't care. If there was a way out, he would find it. But first he had to find Timmy.

Eric and Tracy sat in the dark room, fighting the chilly wind that swept into the gaping hole in their prison wall. Any thought of escaping through the hole was immediately dismissed. With no boat, it would be impossible to swim to land they couldn't even see in the daylight.

But Eric wouldn't sit there helplessly, waiting for whoever was outside that door to decide his and Tracy's fates. The room itself was bare except for the metal filing cabinet, its gray paint chewed through by the saltwater, and that proved to be empty. Immediately, Eric had yanked off his Vasque hiking boots.

Tracy had looked at him as if he'd gone crazy. "I told you, I'm not swimming for it."

But Eric hadn't answered. He'd dug inside the boots, tearing away until he finally worked free the steel arches that the sporting-goods salesman had once chatted on about. After ripping up a section of soggy carpet from the floor, Eric began the slow task of honing the edge of the steel against the exposed cement until they were both as sharp as surgical blades. He'd handed one to Tracy and they'd both waited for their chance.

The wait continued. By sunset, Eric had decided to shave, as he had done every day since the quake. He was one of the few men who still did, most having surrendered to whiskers and long hair. At first, Tracy had tried to imitate Eric's actions by shaving her legs, but the nicks and gouges hadn't proved worth it. Eric had finally convinced her that he actually preferred her with her hair.

What Tracy didn't understand was that Eric shaved not just out of fastidious personal hygiene, as she thought, but out of *fear.*

Fear of what he might become.

He had started to feel it a few months ago. When he was honest with himself, he admitted it had started even before the quakes, back during that first night when Fallows had sent that killer into his home. He had been afraid at first, afraid for his family and for his own life. But that had passed quickly, too quickly, he later realized. In its place had come that adrenaline rush he'd felt in 'Nam when he ran with the Night Shift, the squad of Special Forces assassins that nobody official ever admitted existed. He'd hated the group, and even more their leader, Col. Dirk Fallows. But there were times, too many times, when the power that went with their anonymity pumped through his veins like molten steel. The knowledge that they were sanctioned to do *anything* had disgusted him, yet at the same time exhilarated him. Many of his friends had given in to the power, like walking into a blinding light. They had become cruel and arrogant, as sadistic as their leader. Some had fought it openly, only to die in battle under mysterious circumstances: bullets in the back, sudden grenade attacks. Eric had fought his battle internally.

But now the lure was there again. California was an island cut off from civilization, and as such had become a primitive war zone like 'Nam. The survivors fought for existence, not vague patriotic philosophy. And the struggle permitted any acts, no matter how horrible, all in the name of survival. They were all playing jungle ball.

Eric had felt the power that came with no morality, no boundaries of behavior. The freedom of pure, cruel selfishness. Living in the Void, he called it. And he felt a constant tug, a temptation to become as free as Fallows. He had felt good sometimes in 'Nam, racing with Fallows through a village occupied by Cong, flinging grenades, feeling a heady intoxication as he saw the bodies tumble six feet into the air, their 7.62-mm Chinese Type-50 submachine guns as twisted as their limbs. He had felt invincible, a wisp of wind able to pass through walls or catch bullets in his teeth. He could do anything he wanted, no matter how disgusting, and no one would question him. It was total freedom. But with that freedom came evil. He fought it still, shaving daily to remind himself of who he had been before the quakes. Back when he'd taught history, instead of making it.

What was the sign they found at Jonestown when they discovered the piles of dead bodies? That famous quote from philosopher George Santayana: "Those who cannot remember the past are condemned to repeat it."

His hands were stiffening from the cold wind, but still he scraped the blade along his jaw, edging his scar. He traced the winding pattern, remembering the feel of the hot smoking blade that Fallows had gouged across his face back in 'Nam. His nostrils filled with the sour smell of his own sizzling flesh. He could still see Fallows' grinning face through the puffing smoke of his own seared skin. His blood sissing on the tip of the knife like a drop of water in a frying pan.

"Eric?" Tracy said, dragging him back into the present.

He wiped the cold sweat his memories had produced from his forehead. "Yeah?"

"When we get back to the mainland and write our book about our adventures and the movie studios buy it for millions, who do you think should play me?"

Eric laughed. "How about Goldie Hawn?"

"Nah, too skinny. I was thinking of someone taller, like, uh, Jacqueline Bisset."

"How tall is she?"

"I don't know. But she looks tall."

"But she has an English accent?"

"Yeah, it'll give the whole thing some class.

Maybe I can affect one when I'm doing all the talk shows. 'Bloody good to see you, Merv, ol' boy.' How's that?"

"Lousy."

"I'll work on it."

Eric noticed the strain in Tracy's voice and knew her hip was getting worse. If nothing happened to them by morning, he'd have to use his makeshift blade and cut some of the infection from her wound.

Shadows fractured the bar of light at the bottom of the door as footsteps approached outside. They heard the door being unchained and sat up straight. Tracy slid her sharpened blade into her pants, hooking one curved edge over the top of her panties. The razor edge lay flat against her pubic hairs.

Eric quickly laced up his boots, wedging the steel blade at the hollow next to his ankle.

The door swung open and a crowd of anxious faces peered into the room. Behind them a dim glow from several kerosene lamps cast a shroud of shadows over them disguising their features with flickering splotches of dark. It gave them all sinister hulking looks.

One man emerged from the crowd and stepped into the room, holding a red railroad lantern in one hand and a saber in the other. He was easily six feet four inches with a leather belt worn bandolier style across one shoulder. The empty saber scabbard dangled at his hip. But he also wore a shoulder holster with a .38 Dan Wesson Model 15-2 VH tucked snugly away.

He was about Eric's age, mid-thirties, with light black skin that extended into a little bay at the top of his balding head. He was grinning hugely as he stepped into the middle of the room.

"Wonderful," he smiled, holding the lantern up to see better. "We finally got some poor sonsabitches to walk that damn plank we built." He paused. "Unless you can give us Alabaster's map."

11.

The tall black man leaned on the ornate handle of his saber as if it were a cane. His dark eyes had a mischievous glint to them, but they were deadly serious as they studied Eric and Tracy.

"You were on Rhino's ship," he finally said. "Crew members?"

"Prisoners," Eric answered.

A few people in the crowd laughed skeptically.

The black man smiled. "We've heard that one before, skipper. Care to try a different story?"

Eric didn't respond. His chest ached as if steel claws were shredding their way through skin and bone to grab at his heart. It was taking all of his energy just to maintain consciousness. A glance at Tracy indicated that she wasn't doing much better. But he could see a spark of defiance igniting in her.

"I don't care what you've heard before, pal,"

Tracy said. "We were paddling along on our canoe when they picked us up."

"In your canoe, huh? Like Huck Finn and Tom Sawyer."

"Christ," she sighed in exasperation. "If you used your head as much as your mouth, you'd realize that we couldn't be part of their crew. If we were, why would we have gotten off *The Centurion* in a leaky canoe?" She shifted her hip to show him the wound. "And why would Rhino have shot me?"

The man shrugged. "You got scared when the fighting started. Or you thought the ship would go up in flames. You panicked. Rhino shot you as deserters."

Eric chuckled. "We certainly weren't afraid of the *Home Run* destroying anything but itself."

"What do you mean?"

"Well, first, you set the timer to blow much too soon. Second, the placement of the explosives was all wrong. You had them strung out along the hull instead of in one location. Also, had you built a funnel around them, you could have blown a hole clear through *The Centurion* and probably have sunk her." Eric dismissed them with a disgusted wave of his hand. "All you managed to do was destroy your own ship and get some of your own people killed."

The man frowned. Behind him the crowd discussed Eric's statements in urgent whispers. When the man with the saber spoke again his voice crackled with anger. "Unfortunately we didn't have your expertise. We were just doing our best."

"Unfortunately," Eric nodded.

"We managed to take a couple of them out," a man in the crowd hollered. "Killed one myself." The crowd responded enthusiastically to this.

Before Eric could answer, a young man began elbowing his way through the crowd. Tears of grief and anger streaked his tanned face as he pointed an accusing finger at Eric.

"He killed Teddy," he cried. "I saw him shoot an arrow through him."

"I saw him too," a woman said, grabbing the young man by the shoulders. Eric recognized her as the older woman aboard the *Home Run*.

"What about that?" the black man asked. "Is it true?"

"I did shoot somebody, I don't know who."

"Whose side was he on? Ours or theirs?"

"I couldn't tell."

The black man was incredulous. "You couldn't tell, but you shot him anyway?"

"He shot him," Tracy jumped in, "because the man was burning alive, a human torch, for God's sake. All Eric tried to do was save him a few minutes of agony."

The black man looked at the woman. "Rachel?"

She nodded. "That's the way it looked to me, Blackjack. I just wanted to hear it to be certain."

Blackjack stared at Eric and Tracy, pinching absently at the whiskered skin under his chin. Finally he turned his back and started out the door. "Bring them along," he ordered.

"This might sound selfish," Blackjack smiled, passing the canteen to Tracy, "but the quakes are the best thing that could have happened to me."

Tracy swigged the warm water, swallowing greedily. When she finished, she wiped the excess water from her chin with her palm and said, "Care to explain?"

"Maybe." Blackjack's smile widened, displaying more teeth. "If you live."

The three of them were sitting in the middle of a huge room the size of a warehouse that once had been the busy main floor of stockbrokers Finch, Levy, and Treemont. The overworked office staff had snidely referred to it as LAX Annex, calling the path that ran down the middle of the room between the rows of cubicles, The Runway. The Runway continued out of the main room down a corridor, passed the Xerox room, the Conference Room, the Executive Lounge, and finally halted at the private offices of Finch, Levy, and Treemont. Seven years ago Treemont had convinced his partners to take offices in this building because it was quakeproof. He'd been right; hardly any damage had been done to it from the shock of the quakes. However, Treemont, a short stubby man who'd only recently begun to battle his "blossoming behind," as his wife called it, by three-times-a-week workouts on Nautilus equipment, had been trampled to death on The Runway after the second quake. Forty-three full-time employees, herded together with twelve part-timers and a Xerox repairwoman, had each contributed a footprint or two to the crushed body. Finch had tried to help his partner, but had been too late. The third partner, Levy, had actually been one of the first to stomp on Treemont in his own dash to the exit. Not that it mattered. None of the partners was alive by the end of the day.

The office had originally been designed to house fifty desks, each partitioned off to form semiprivate cubicles, each with its own telephone and video terminal plugged into the company's vast digital computer system. The interior designer had assured the partners that this setup would provide a sense of privacy yet still give the employees the feeling they were being watched. "Guaranteed maximum efficiency," the designer had winked.

The screens were all gone now, neatly stacked against the far wall as if the building's new residents thought they might someday come in handy again. Each little cubicle had a blanket or a flap of carpet hanging down to close it off from the rest and to form tiny apartments. The desks remained, serving triple duty as dressers, dining tables, and sometimes beds for the children. Behind a few partitions, Eric could see a lantern casting a silhouette on the sheet or blanket that was both door and wall. A few feet away, he saw the outline of a woman breast-feeding her hungry baby.

Despite the ventilation provided by the shattered glass, the room still was heavy with the smell of unwashed bodies and smoke from the lanterns. Eric didn't mind the odor, having endured far worse in 'Nam. Curiously, the smell of these bodies was different than those on *The Centurion*. Orientals claim they can barely stand the smell of Americans due to their heavy consumption of meat, compared with the lighter eastern diets of fish and vegetables. That lighter scent was what Eric smelled here, earthy but sweet. He realized for the first time how healthy and well fed they all looked, though he'd seen no animals. They must catch a hell of a lot of fish, he thought.

"Can you think of any reason why we should let you live?" Blackjack asked. The three of them were sitting in his cubicle. The ratty beach towel with CALIFORNIA: A STATE OF MIND printed in electric blue over a smiling surfer was flipped open so the two armed guards could watch Eric and Tracy closely. The woman held a spear, the man a compound bow. Blackjack casually continued, "Any reason we shouldn't toss you back into the ocean, *sans* canoe?"

"I can't see any advantage to killing us," Eric responded, just as casually.

"Christ," Tracy said. "Listen to you two. We're talking about *killing*, goddamn it. And you two sound as if you were discussing a garage sale."

"She's right, of course," Blackjack agreed. "It is so uncivilized. But that doesn't change anything. As Walter Cronkite used to say, 'That's the way it is.' As far as I can see, you two are damaged goods." He pointed at Tracy's nasty hip wound. "In her condition, she wouldn't bring me much at an auction. And you, sport . . ." He nodded at Eric's chest. The blood had soaked through the bandages and blotted through his shirt. "You aren't exactly fit."

"We'll take care of ourselves," Eric said. "Just give us back our canoe and the duct tape, and we'll be out of your way."

His eyes narrowed on Eric. "Duct tape? To fix a canoe."

"It'll keep the water out long enough for us to reach shore."

"Then what? She can't travel by foot, her hip's in pretty bad condition."

"I'll take care of it."

The man laughed. "How? With spit and duct tape?"

"There are many possibilities," Eric said quietly. "Yarrow is a standard treatment, used by both the ancient Greeks and knights of the Middle Ages for battle-wound dressings. Comfrey root and marshmallow root poultices could work, along with some plantain tea taken internally. Horsetail stems, garlic, pot marigold, chamomile, flax seed. There's a whole pharmacy growing out there. One-stop shopping, no waiting at the check-out stand."

"Tell him about the maggots," Tracy added.

"First explosives, now medicine," Blackjack said. "Any other talents?"

Tracy knew Eric wouldn't answer, so she answered for him, turning to face the armed female guard as she spoke. "Just some advice for your women. Sphagnum moss can be wrapped in cloth and used as sanitary napkins." It was something Eric had taught her. At the time she'd been embarrassed that he'd known how to take care of her body better than she had. But it had also touched her deeply that he'd been thoughtful enough to do so. Tracy turned back to Blackjack. "Now, we've proven we're no threat to you, and we've given you information. So there's no need to keep us prisoners here, is there?"

Blackjack leaned his long body against the flimsy partition. On the other side, they heard somebody snoring. "What can you tell us about *The Centurion?*"

Tracy shrugged. "What do you want to know?"

"Everything."

Tracy looked at Eric.

"It's a seventy-three-foot staysail Schooner," Eric began, taking another gulp of water from the canteen, capping it, and tossing it back to Blackjack, who caught it with one hand. Eric's lips curled in what might have been mistaken for a smile. "The interiors are teak. Very fancy. It's got three double staterooms and a large salon, two heads, and a nifty galley. The

130

planking is three-inch fir over three-inch and six-inch fit frames on sixteen-inch centers. The inner hull consists of alternating three-inch and six-inch planking. It's got two dinghies and a seven and a half kilowatt Onan generator to power its searchlights. The engine is a GM 6-71 diesel. I don't know whether it's fueled or not."

"Finally something you *don't* know," Blackjack sighed.

"Gets to you, doesn't it?" Tracy added.

Blackjack leaned forward, hovering over Tracy with his lantern. "Let me take a look at that wound."

"Why?"

He smiled. "I was a doctor. Still am, I guess, technically. Dr. Fennimore Cohen, but now I'm called Blackjack. Like the card game. Made it up myself. Can't be a pirate without a nickname, they won't take you seriously. Like professional sports."

"You're a pirate?" Tracy asked, startled. "Like Rhino and his gang."

"They're our number one competitor. For now."

Tracy shook her head. "But all these people, these families. Children, for Christ's sake. You can't be like him."

"Well, we're a little different. We're more of a community." He spread his hands to indicate the whole floor. "But otherwise, there's no difference."

"We're *nothing* like Rhino and those pigs," the woman guard spat.

Blackjack looked up at her with a frown. "You're wrong, Belinda. We are just like them. We rob other ships that cross our waterways, we trade goods at Liar's Cove with the other thieves and crooks. Maybe we aren't as bloodthirsty as the others, but that's not much of a difference in the long run. And we do kill when necessary. Let's not kid ourselves about who we are and what we do. We aren't noble outlaws." He let his hard gaze fall on Eric and Tracy. "It wouldn't be wise to confuse us with Robin Hood."

"No chance," Tracy said immediately.

"Good. Then you won't hesitate to tell me all you know about Alabaster's map." Blackjack kept his glare fixed on them a moment longer, the flame from the railroad lantern reflecting in his dark eyes.

"We don't know anything about Alabaster or any damn map," she said.

Blackjack ignored the words, returning to administer to Tracy's hip, spreading apart the torn pants so he could examine the wound. "I was a pediatrician, but I thought two years in ER prepared me for just about anything. Until the quakes."

"Here, let me loosen this so you can see better." Tracy unfastened the button to her jeans and began tugging at the zipper. Blackjack looked slightly embarrassed, glancing over at Eric, who was already shifting in preparation for what he knew would come next.

Tracy plucked the honed sliver of steel from

her panties and pressed the razor edge of the blade against Blackjack's throat. He started to back away and she grabbed a handful of hair at the back of his head. "No, no," she warned, her voice pitched to a high squeak from the excitement. "Don't move, Dr. Pirate. This is the first time I've ever done anything like this, and I might make a terrible mistake and slit your throat."

"Okay, okay," Blackjack whispered. "Easy does it."

Eric was on his feet, taking the weapons from the startled guards. He motioned toward Blackjack, and they walked toward their leader. "Sit," he ordered. They did.

"Not bad, huh," Tracy said excitedly, looking at Eric.

"Keep your eye on *him*, not me," Eric said.

"Yeah, right." She turned back, clutching Blackjack's hair even harder. "But not bad, huh?"

"Pretty good."

"Whatta ya mean, 'pretty good.' Damn good."

"No. Damn good would have been if you'd waited until he finished treating your leg. After all, he is a doctor, remember?"

Tracy sighed. "Right."

Eric snatched the .38 from Blackjack's shoulder holster and held it on the three prisoners while Tracy used the spear to climb to her feet. "But otherwise, you did a hell of a job."

Tracy looked at him with a wide grin. "Damn

right I did."

Eric handed her the .38, hooked the guard's quiver of arrows onto his pants and crooked a finger at Blackjack. "This way, Doctor."

Blackjack stood up, still massaging his throat where Tracy's blade had shaved off a few whiskers. No matter how much he rubbed, he could still feel the blade pressing against his skin. "There's no place to go. You can't get through this room without one of the other guards spotting you. Just take your damn canoe and duct tape and go."

"What's to stop you from coming after us?" Eric asked. "Our canoe is no match for your ship."

Blackjack laughed. "Why should we bother? You have nothing we want."

"Not even Alabaster's map?"

Blackjack fought to keep his face expressionless, but the eyes flared at Eric's question. "Do you have it?"

"How could we?" Eric asked. "You had us searched."

Blackjack glanced at the steel blades hooked in Tracy and Eric's jeans pockets. "You're a little more clever than we expected."

Eric liked it that Blackjack didn't make excuses or try to place blame. He could have yelled at Belinda, who'd first captured and searched Tracy and Eric. But he didn't. He stood there and tried to keep everyone calm. Defuse the situation, they'd called it during Eric's training for the Night Shift. Pirate or Warlord,

134

in some ways it was all the same job.

"Let's go," Eric said.

"What about Alabaster's map?" Blackjack demanded.

"We don't know anything about it, except that Rhino and Angel were as anxious to get it as you are."

"Damn!" he cursed, turning to Belinda and the other guard seated at his feet. "That means we've only got one chance to find out where the map is. And even that looks slim."

Tracy nodded to Eric. "Look, none of this concerns us. Shouldn't we be getting the hell out of here?"

"Absolutely." He nudged Blackjack ahead of them out onto The Runway, glancing over his shoulder at the seated unarmed guards. "There's no point in following us yet. It'll just make us nervous and put the doctor here in more jeopardy." Having said that, he ushered Blackjack and Tracy across the room, knowing they'd be followed all the way. Tracy used the spear as a cane, limping and hopping painfully. Every few steps they stopped for her to catch her breath.

Outside the Long Beach Halo, the sun was beginning to rise, bright and cheerful on the rest of the world. Inside the Halo, sunrise was distinguished by smoky orange fingers creeping over the horizon like a skin infection.

As they walked, guards posted at the broken glass openings turned their weapons on the trio, only to be waved back by Blackjack. Eric noted

135

Belinda and the other guard following at a discreet distance. Both had rearmed themselves along the way.

The Runway led straight to the elevator. Around the corner was an exit sign and door marked STAIRS.

"Through here," Eric said.

Blackjack shook his head. "What's the point? Your canoe is back at the other end. We'll give it to you. Believe me, right now I'll be happy just to see you two paddling away."

"What's to stop you from putting a bullet or arrow in our backs then?"

"What for? Why waste the ammunition?"

"I don't know. Pride, maybe. You're pirates, remember?"

Tracy watched the exchange without comment. She knew Eric had something on his mind and they wouldn't leave until he'd been satisfied. And apparently that meant her hobbling up the stairs.

They pushed through the door, Tracy bracing herself on the railing holding the .38 on Blackjack while Eric jammed the spear against the door, keeping the others outside.

"You're wasting your time," Blackjack said, his voice echoing in the stairwell. "There's nothing interesting up there."

"Then why aren't some of your people living up there?"

"The roof has holes in it. We'd all die of exposure."

136

"Sounds reasonable. Let's check it out."

Tracy pulled herself along the railing, taking each step with great difficulty. Eric wrapped his arms around her waist and boosted her along. They both glanced over the railing, down the stairwell, and saw the cold dark water only half a story below.

Blackjack walked in front of them, his long legs comfortably taking two steps at a time.

"Not so fast," Tracy said, rapping the gun butt on the railing to get his attention. They could hear the door below them rattling as the guards tried to force it open.

Blackjack waited nervously for them as Eric lifted Tracy up the last few steps. Thick drops of sweat rolled down her face from the effort, dripped from her chin and nose. The hip wound had started to bleed again.

Downstairs the sharp crack of splintering wood echoed up the stairwell. The mop-handle spear shattered and the door banged open.

"You first," Eric gestured to Blackjack. The doctor reached for the door to the top floor, twisted the handle, and pulled it open.

Footsteps clattered against the metal steps like prisoners rattling tin cups on bars.

The three of them shoved through the door into the top floor, locking the door behind them.

Tracy looked around with awe, spinning on her one good leg, her mouth hanging open. "Impossible," she said, shaking her head.

Eric stared, a small smile tugging at his lips.

"How did you do all this?" Tracy finally asked.

"Hard work."

Eric smiled. "I thought you were a pirate?"

"I am," Blackjack said.

"According to this," Eric circled one hand as if he were twirling a lasso, "you're more of a farmer."

"Looks can be deceiving."

They walked slowly down the long rows while beefy shoulders slammed into the locked door, trying to bash it in.

The entire floor had been reconstructed into one giant room, and that one room was now a full greenhouse. The roof had been chipped and chiseled away, then recovered with glass and plastic awkwardly patched together in a bizarre mosaic. Yet it accomplished its task, providing protection against the cold ocean wind while allowing the orange sunlight to pour into the room.

The room itself was flourishing with greenery, thick with foliage, and heavy with the rich musky smell of moist soil. Row after row of sandboxlike partitions lined the room, each sprouting different plants. Tomatoes, squash, potatoes, even orange and lemon trees. Against the far wall were ten towering water tanks, each the size of a large hospital elevator.

Eric kneeled beside one of the boxes and snatched a bulging tomato from a stem. He polished it against his shirt, then tossed it to

Tracy with a grin. She caught it, immediately biting into it. Red goo and slimy seeds squirted across her cheeks, but she didn't care. She chewed with her eyes closed like an adolescent girl imagining a romantic interlude with her favorite movie star. Before she'd finished chewing her first bite, she bit off another mouthful. Tomato innards dripped onto her pants. "God, we're back in Eden at last," she said with her mouth stuffed full. "I knew there'd been some bureaucratic mix-up the first time."

Eric plucked another ripe tomato for himself and ate it in three bites. He was still chewing the last mouthful when the door exploded off its hinges and a dozen armed guards burst into the room, their weapons swinging toward him.

"What exactly do you want to know?" Blackjack asked.

Eric tapped the barrel of his .38 against his palm. What indeed?

The three of them were sitting back in Blackjack's cubicle, the ratty beach towel with the faded surfer on it flapped down to provide a little privacy. Outside the cubicle, a dozen armed guards stood milling around, waiting to hear Eric use the gun on their leader or to see him just keep waltzing up and down the stairs with a gun to Blackjack's head.

"How'd you go about construction? That's the biggest damn greenhouse I've ever seen."

Blackjack held up his hands and shook his

head. "Let's get that straight right now, man. I had nothing to do with its conception or construction. Had I been around here then I'd have told them they were all nuts. But the guy who brainstormed it was a skinny guy named Daniel Loeb. Used to be an engineer for Fluor Corporation, then ditched the whole thing to join the Peace Corps back in the 'sixties. Remember back then when everybody thought they could actually make a difference? Well, ol' Daniel Loeb was the kind of guy who didn't know the 'sixties ended more than fifteen years ago. He completely missed the Me Decade." Blackjack pulled open the bottom drawer of his desk.

Eric's fist immediately pushed the gun toward Blackjack's head. "Careful."

"Hey, easy, man. No weapons." He dipped his hand into the bottom drawer that once held Shirley Pinto's note pad, extra staples, a box of floppy disks for her IBM word processor, the latest James Michener novel which she read over lunch, a container of diet pills to help her drop fifteen pounds so she could fit into her swimsuit by summer, and an extra pair of Leggs pantyhose because she lived in mortal fear of running hers and having the other girls laugh at her. On the way home from the first quake, she stopped to help an elderly couple who shot her in the face and stole her Datsun.

When Blackjack's hands reappeared, they were clutching three small oranges the size of tangerines. He grinned, juggled them for a minute, then reeled each in, tossing one each to Tracy and Eric, keeping the third for himself. "Home grown," he said as Tracy tore the peels from her orange like someone frantically unwrapping a present. "Remember when 'home grown' used to refer to marijuana? If nothing else, these quakes sure put things in perspective, eh?"

"What about Daniel Loeb?" Eric reminded him.

"Yeah, right. Well, Loeb returned from the Peace Corps and became a rabbi. No shit. Had a reformed congregation and a temple over in Fountain Valley. After the California blitz, Loeb turned a group of survivors into a farming community."

"Like a religious cult?" Tracy asked.

"No. They could worship whoever or whatever they wanted. Loeb didn't care. They had goats and cows for milk, but the rest of their food they grew themselves. Even had avocado and nut trees. Amazing."

Tracy had eaten her orange and was gnawing on the insides of the peels. "Come on, Doctor, get to the point."

"You can't keep word of something like that secret for long. Marauders came down and slaughtered most of the settlers, drove the others off. But that doesn't stop Loeb. He remembers hearing about these half-submerged buildings from some of his people at camp, and leads the survivors out here. What could be a better defense than the whole damned Pacific Ocean?

141

Like a giant moat around their castle. So he moves the settlement out to this building and starts his farming community again. This time, nobody even knows about the food."

Eric stood up, reached into the bottom drawer of the desk and picked out two more oranges. He dropped one in Tracy's lap and sat back down, his legs crossed. Blackjack gave him an annoyed look, but Eric just smiled and began peeling the orange in one spiraling unbroken peel.

"Anyway," Blackjack continued, slamming the desk drawer closed, "the only drawback was they had to haul the fresh water all the way out here for the settlers and the crops. That made them vulnerable to pirates. And in these waters that meant Rhino." He pointed at the gun Eric was aiming at him while he peeled his orange. "Is that necessary? You might slip and shoot me accidentally."

Eric smiled.

Blackjack continued, "So Loeb was making a water run with one of his ships and they were stopped by Rhino and Angel. Loeb had purposely made sure there were no women on these runs so pirates wouldn't have anything to sell. But he didn't understand Rhino. He'll attack just to be doing something. The man's a perpetual motion machine, can't rest, can't sit still. It's like he's on speed twenty-four hours a day. Well, he caught up with Loeb's water barge and sank it."

"And Loeb?" Eric asked.

"Sank him too. He personally cut off Loeb's arms and threw him into the water. It was all over in a few minutes."

Tracy stopped eating her orange. "Christ."

"And his death left you in charge here?" Eric asked.

Blackjack laughed. "Hardly. I told you, I'm a pirate, not a martyr. I have my own Wellington 63 yacht I bought back when I was a doctor and a medical corporation. Some of the crew are former hospital staff, others I picked up along the way. Not Rhino's type of crew, but they're loyal and know how to fight." He gestured over at his saber which was leaning against the wall. "A gift from the crew. Nifty, huh?"

"So who's in charge around here?"

"Daniel Loeb was survived by a wife, as they say in the papers. Rachel Loeb. She was in charge of the suicide mission on board the *Home Run*. She figured she could get close enough to destroy Rhino once and for all."

Eric pried a segment of orange and reached it to Tracy, who'd already gobbled hers down. She popped the segment in her mouth, chewing and saying thank you at the same time. Eric swept the room with his gun. "And just where do you fit in to all this?"

"Bodyguard," Blackjack smiled happily. "I was hired by Rachel Loeb to protect them on their water runs. She'd heard about me, for Chrissakes. Can you dig it, we have a god-damned *reputation*. Like Yul Brynner in *The*

Magnificent Seven, remember? We even have the same hairstyle. I love it." He ran his hand over his balding pate, chuckling like a kid describing his first Little League home run. "In return we get all the food we want and a safe harbor. In a straight head-on fight with Rhino and his crew, my people don't have a chance. His ship's faster and his crew's a lot more ruthless, but we make it unprofitable for him to risk a battle. For what? Some water, a few women?"

"Then he doesn't know about the farming?"

"Nope. He just thinks we scavenge the land and bring our booty over the water, using the building as a hideout. But he's not dumb, neither is that Angel lady with him. Eventually they'll figure it out. Then we'll be in serious trouble."

Eric dragged the barrel of the gun along his scar, the metal cool as it skidded over the bumps in his skin. "So who the hell is Alabaster and what's his map for?"

Blackjack frowned, his dark face suddenly darker in the wavering light of the lamp. He lifted the bell jar from the lantern, licked his fingertips, and pinched the wick. The flame sissed against his wet skin, then vanished in a stream of smoke like a circus magician. The orange sheen of daylight squeezed through the cracks and seams of the cubicle. Outside they could hear the sounds of people starting their day. Blackjack stood up and waved a hand for Tracy and Eric to follow. "I guess you're ready to know about Alabaster too."

"This is Nurse Hatchet," Blackjack said.

"Havczech," the woman corrected, obviously used to his teasing. She adjusted the too-tight running suit that stretched over her plump figure like the skin of an overripe plum.

"Joyce was a school nurse for twenty-three years at Claremont Junior High School. She's seen it all."

"I thought I had," she grumbled, "till I saw the likes of you. Imagine, a doctor of medicine running around with a silly sword hanging on his hip." She shook her head and clucked her tongue. "Probably hit your head goin' through the Pirates of the Caribbean ride at Disneyland. That's the only explanation."

"You think I *like* being a pirate? Hell, I'm doing this for black folk everywhere. Breaking the racial barrier in maritime endeavors. The goddamn Jackie Robinson of piracy." He laughed, patted her ample behind, which she ignored with another shake of her head and cluck of her tongue. "How's the patient?" he asked quietly, his voice suddenly grim.

The nurse shrugged her rounded shoulders. "Steady."

They followed her across the room, Tracy limping and using another spear as a cane. The room was once the office of the three partners Levy, Treemont, and Finch, but was now the settlement's hospital. The walls had been torn down to provide more space. The "beds" were nothing more than folded blankets, sheets, towels, and, in some cases, rags piled on the floor in the shape of a bed. Surgical instruments were nothing more than a variety of sharpened kitchen utensils and cosmetic paraphernalia. A metal bookcase against the wall contained some medicines, but the supplies were sparse.

There were three patients in the hospital. The first was a young toddler named Mark with stomach cramps. While the parents had been upstairs working the soil, they'd left their sixteen-year-old daughter, Tammy, to babysit with Mark. Tammy had slipped away for just a few minutes of heavy petting with Phil Rubin over behind where that Piper Cub had crashed. But Phil had wanted more than a little French kissing, so to keep him satisfied, she'd let him fondle her breasts a couple of extra minutes. By the time she'd returned, little Mark had eaten a few unidentified bugs, the severed black legs of one still riding his lower lip.

The second patient was an ancient woman in her nineties. She was terribly frail, sharp bones poking at gray skin, and looked like a deflated doll. Her eyes were open, but she didn't seem to see anything. Her lips quivered as if she were speaking, but no sound came out.

"Lila is the center of controversy around here," Blackjack explained as they approached her. "She's bedridden, senile, and rarely lucid, but she still eats her share of food and drinks plenty of water. And she needs occasional medication. As you can see, these supplies aren't very ample."

"So they don't know whether to keep feeding her," Tracy said, "or toss her out the window."

"That's about it."

"What's Rachel Loeb say?" Eric asked.

"What you'd expect a rabbi's wife to say."

"And you?"

"None of my business. I'm just a hired gun." But as they passed Lila's shriveled body, Blackjack stooped over and tucked the bedding around her shoulders. She didn't seem to notice.

The last patient was a young woman in her early twenties.

"Worst case of exposure I've ever seen," Blackjack whispered as they approached.

Eric looked into her face and was surprised she was still alive. Its skin was blistered into crusty flakes and scabs. He thought a slight breeze might blow her whole face away. Her lips were swollen, baked into black strips resembling bark. She breathed through her mouth, the air raspy as it puffed in and out. Her eyes were open slightly, and seemed to perk up a bit when she saw Blackjack.

"You look much better, Christine. No, no, don't talk anymore. Just rest. Nurse Hatchet will look after you."

She moved her lips, but nothing came out.

"He's fine, Christine. Resting in another room. We want to keep him isolated to reduce risk of infection. You just worry about yourself for now, okay?"

Christine blinked her eyes in response.

Mark Sterling woke up from his nap and started to cry.

"Coming, Mark," Nurse Havczech said and waddled over to him.

Blackjack gestured with his head for them to follow him. They went through a door at the back of the room which led to the executive conference room where the three partners had held court every Tuesday morning at 11:00 A.M., delivering notes on how to improve office profitability. The image they most liked was that they were coaching their team on to the World Series. However, today the office was empty, except for a body lying in the middle of the conference table with a beach towel draped over it. The rancid smell hit them like a blast furnace. Tracy cupped her hand over her mouth and nose.

Blackjack grabbed the edges of the towel and with the exaggerated flourish of a master chef, swept the towel off the body. *Voilà*. Flounder á la Alabaster."

"Eric," Tracy said, forgetting the smell a moment as she leaned closer to the body. "That's the guy. He's the one."

There was no mistaking the doughy skin, the half-eaten face, the hole through the skull where Eric had pried loose the stubborn arrow. It was the man he'd fished out of the ocean last night. It was Alabaster.

* * *

They were standing next to the Piper Cub where Tammy Sterling had had her breasts massaged by Phil Rubin while her little brother bit bugs in half. The plane was wedged tight into the building.

"It was here when the others arrived," Blackjack explained. "No one knows what happened to the pilot or why it crashed. There was a little fuel in it, but they drained it long ago. I guess as long as it plugs the hole, they'll just leave it there." He patted the plane's fuselage. "This is one of the few places we can talk and not be overheard. Some of what I'm going to tell you only Rachel and I know."

"So why isn't she here?" Tracy asked. She was still limping, but the medication and bandage Nurse Havczech had provided reduced the pain.

"Rachel tends to the farming and daily life of the community. She says security is up to me."

"She didn't feel that way when she rigged the *Home Run* to blow," Eric reminded him.

Blackjack forgot about Eric's gun for a moment and stepped angrily toward him. "I tried to talk her out of it, told her I'd do it. But she insisted, said that if it didn't work the settlement would need me more than it would her. She's nuts, man."

Eric could see he'd probed a nerve, that Blackjack's feelings about Rachel Loeb were deeper than he wanted to admit. He changed the subject. "Tell me about Alabaster. What's the fuss about his map?"

Blackjack removed a small leather pouch

from his pants pocket and a packet of Zig-Zag cigarette papers. Deftly he sprinkled some of the contents of the pouch on the paper, spit-sealed it, and lit it with an almost-empty Bic lighter. He inhaled deeply, held the smoke in his chest for a long minute, his eyes blinking rapidly as if he were in some pain, then exhaled the sweet smoke at the Piper Cub. "BLACK EX-DOCTOR DOPE FIEND PIRATE." He smiled, sweeping his hand across the air as if under-lining a newspaper headline. He shook his head. "If we ever get off this island, we're going to spend the first six months just being interviewed by reporters. *Ebony* magazine's going to be disappointed in me." He looked at Tracy and Eric as he expected some disapprov-ing remark.

Neither said anything. Eric had never really gotten a foothold in the drug culture of his peers. He'd popped a few uppers in college, smoked some grass to be sociable at parties, ingested an LSD sugar cube because he was curious. The uppers had given him a headache; the pot had only made his tongue taste dry and trampled-on; the LSD had been one pleasant euphoric dream, none of the screaming demons he'd expected to encounter. Nevertheless, he avoided all—how did the cops put it now?—"controlled substances," not so much out of disapproval, as out of fear. Fear that he would not be in total control of himself when he needed to be.

There it was. That word. Control. Annie had

often accused him of wanting to control every situation, even harmless social gatherings. "Not overtly," she'd complained after one Sunday brunch with some of her friends from jazzercize class. "Just somehow, even when you don't say anything for hours, we all get the feeling we're doing just what you want us to. Oh, hell, I'm being silly."

But she was right. He scrutinized everyone, no matter how subtle and smiling he tried to be. And eventually most wilted under his gaze, as if they feared he had discovered a terrible secret about them. Their friends had been few, a fact that sometimes disturbed Annie, who'd been brought up to be a much more social creature. "Even without saying anything," she'd said, "you ask too much of people. You judge them." But the friends they'd cultivated over the years were fiercely loyal, the way Eric thought they should be.

Blackjack leaned against the fuselage of the Piper Cub and slid his back along the metal hull until he was sitting on the ground, flicking the ashes from his joint on a jagged piece of glass at his feet. Eric helped Tracy to sit, arranging her legs so the hip was less painful.

"You remember," Blackjack began, "when the cops and military got together after the first quake and did their door-to-door thing? Confiscated everybody's guns because of all the looting and panicking neighbors shooting each other."

Eric saw the jeep parked outside his house, the men brandishing rifles on his doorstep;

151

Annie and the kids frightened; Eric's crusty old mother demanding proof of their authorization, studying the piece of paper they reluctantly handed her as Eric arrived. All dead now. Except Timmy.

"I remember," Eric nodded.

"Well, all those guns and ammunition were sent to secret stockpile locations where they were heavily guarded. Even though they'd given receipts for the weapons and promised to return them after the situation returned to normal, orders had come down to destroy all the guns. They managed to do just that at most of the stockpiles. But not all." He took another deep drag on his joint, sucking air between his teeth. A think film of sweat had popped out along his forehead. "Each one of those stockpiles contained enough firepower to start a small army. And considering the state of most the weaponry on this island right now, whoever gets ahold of those caches could storm across California and rule it anyway they see fit."

"Things are tough enough around here without that kind of thing," Tracy said.

"Damn right, lady. But business is business, at least that's the way Alabaster saw it. He was a computer programmer who was also in the National Guard. His unit had been called up after the first quake and he was assigned as one of the guards at a weapons stockpile. When the next quakes hit, everyone at the stockpile was killed."

"Except Alabaster," Eric said. "And he made

152

a map."

"Yeah. He hid them all at a new location, just in case anyone was alive who knew about the stockpile. He was the only one who knew where all those glorious weapons were. He didn't have the stomach or ambition to use them himself in a conquering march across California, but he knew there were plenty of others who'd gladly take up the banner. He approached Rhino."

"I'll bet he did," Eric said. "And Rhino probably peed his pants at the thought of all those guns."

Blackjack laughed. "He does run around like a nervous poodle with a jet up his ass. I've seen some cases of manic depression in medical school, and treated hyperactive children at the hospital, but I've never seen anything quite like Rhino. He's like an overwound spring."

"Do you think he wanted the guns for himself or to sell them to someone else?" Tracy asked.

"I'd guess he was going to use them himself. He'd recruit an army, arm them, and start at one end of the state and march lengthwise until he was King of California. He'd do it just to keep his mind and body occupied while it was moving. But he'd also enjoy it." Blackjack inhaled another lungful of smoke, tapped the end of the joint against the chip of glass until the butt was dead. He slipped the rest into his pocket. "But according to Mrs. Alabaster back in the hospital, her husband's boat was attacked while they were on their way to meet Rhino. Alabaster was killed, but she managed to hang

153

on to a life jacket for a couple days. We picked her up two days ago. Found Alabaster's body last night."

"Must have been soon after we were picked up by Rhino's ship." Eric tapped the gun absently against his palm. "But if Rhino doesn't have the map, who does?"

Blackjack's lip arced smugly. "Alabaster may have been a whiz with computers, but when it came to dealing with badasses, he was one dumb white boy. Christine Alabaster filled us in on most of the details." Blackjack laughed again, but coldly, without humor. "That lumpy doughboy Rhino wants that map *so bad*. And he doesn't know how close it is."

Eric stared at Blackjack, letting his eyes rake the black man's expression. He understood. "Rhino was double-crossed. He didn't know Alabaster was dead. Someone from his own ship went out a couple days early to meet Alabaster, kill him, and steal the map. Then the double-crosser pretended to be confused when Alabaster didn't show up for the meeting. That's the person with the map. And there's only one person on that ship with enough brains, guts, and arrogance to outsmart Rhino. Angel."

Blackjack looked surprised. "You know her?"

"Enough to know that her nickname is short for Angel of Mercy, a cruel irony that street people in Vietnam thought appropriate. She always got what she wanted, most of the time through personal torture of reluctant business associates. She used a balisong knife and knew just where to cut." He winced remembering when they'd found a whimpering heap of a person she'd just finished with. Lying facedown in a puddle of blood, he was paralyzed from the neck down, almost drowning in his own blood. His exposed spine was slashed with cross-hatches from neck to buttocks. Two of the soldiers with Eric had thrown up. The man begged them to kill him, but orders required he be brought back for interrogation. Col. Dirk Fallows had backed the jeep up to the door as they loaded the man into the back. "That damn woman is a regular Veg-o-matic." Fallows had grinned, making his voice deep like a TV huckster's. "She slices, she dices, she juliennes."

Tracy reached out to Blackjack. "Give me a hit." She inhaled the smoke like a college girl puffing her first cigarette, coughed, handed the joint back. She cleared her throat to speak. "Never could get the hang of it. And if ever there was a time to be flat-on-your-ass stoned, this is it."

"As a former doctor," Blackjack said, sucking in another gallon of smoke, his voice pinched as he tried to speak and keep the smoke in at the same time, "I have to warn you that smoking can be hazardous to your health."

Tracy laughed, the sudden movement detonating land mines of pain in her hip. She gritted her teeth, tears welling in her eyes.

"So according to Christine Alabaster," Eric continued, "Angel has the map to the stockpile of weapons. But we know that Rhino is unaware of her little treachery. He's still out there searching for Alabaster."

"Right. That's why Rachel insisted we try to blow them up right away. It doesn't matter whether Rhino or Angel eventually gets the weapons. Whoever gets them, it will be bad for this settlement . . . not to mention the rest of California." He hesitated, stared directly at Eric. "But if *we* had the weapons, we could at least fight back against any marauders. These people could move back to the land and live like humans, not water rats."

"So you want the map too?" Eric said.

"Yes. To defend ourselves."

Eric looked at Tracy. "How do you feel?"

"Okay. Actually, the hip's better. Probably be good as new in a couple days."

Blackjack shook his head. "You'll be able to walk without a cane in a week or two," he said, then hesitated, tapping the burning end of the joint against the hunk of glass. "But you won't be as good as new. You'll probably limp slightly for the rest of your life."

Eric didn't say anything, nor did he move toward her. This kind of knowledge needed to be absorbed alone. He had suspected the bullet had chipped off a bit too much bone, mashed too many nerves.

"What?" Tracy smiled, as if she really hadn't heard him or had thought he was joking. She had the look of most people when told they had a permanent disability, no matter how minor.

156

The pale gaze of disbelief, the ashen expression as all of their confidence drained out of their bodies. If one thing could go wrong, then anything might. Their aura of invincibility was shattered forever.

"It might have been worse," Blackjack explained. "You might have lost the leg."

Tracy glared at the bandage on her hip, then suddenly tore it off as if that were the cause of her injury. "Goddamn it," she screamed. "Goddamn this place." She threw the bloody bandage in Blackjack's face. He didn't try to stop her, nor did he protect himself. He let it hit, leaving a spongy splotch of her blood on his forehead. The bandage tumbled down his chest and onto the ground. He picked it up, crawled over to Tracy, and silently reattached the bandage. She let him.

"What do you want from us?" Eric asked Blackjack while he was hunched over Tracy's hip.

"Huh?"

"You didn't tell us all this just for friendly conversation. You want something."

Blackjack tucked the flaps of Tracy's pants over her bandage and looked up at Eric. "I know who you are, Ravensmith. I didn't at first, but Rachel recognized you from the news on TV. When you testified at Fallows' trial. I know a little bit about your background. I don't mean the history professor jazz, I mean that Night Shift stuff in 'Nam. No matter how much I act like a pirate, I know a hell of a lot more about

157

medicine. But you know about soldiering, I mean *real* fighting. And we could use you for what we have in mind."

"Just what do you have in mind?"

He rocked back on his heels and hugged his knees, his dark eyes shining with intensity. "We've got to figure Rhino will need to recruit a few more crew members after what we did to him earlier. And he'll want to try to pick up a line on Alabaster. There's only one place he can go to do both. Liar's Cove. A little fortress of scum where anything goes. At Liar's Cove there is no law, and nothing is too weird or kinky."

"Get to the point."

"I figure that's where Angel will try to slip away and recruit her own crew, then head for the weapons." He picked up a loose screw from the cement floor, threw it out the broken window next to the Piper. A second later they heard the splash. "I want to go to Liar's Cove and kidnap Angel. We get the map from her and find the weapons ourselves."

"Jesus," Tracy said. "Talk about limping for the rest of your life. Your brain must be limping along on one cylinder."

Eric's lips twisted into a grim smile. "And what do we get out of it if we agree?"

"Eric!" Tracy said.

Encouraged, Blackjack leaned closer, speaking quickly like a conspirator assuring a reluctant ally that the alarm systems have been cut. "You can have your pick of the weapons. All both of you can carry. And passage to wherever you want. You must have been heading somewhere in that canoe. We'll deliver you there in our ship. Safe and sound. And heavily armed."

Eric stood up, offered a hand to Tracy. He pulled her to her feet and handed her the spear for a cane. They started walking back toward The Runway, Blackjack trailing behind them.

"We'll think about it," Eric said.

"Sure, that's all I ask."

"California," Tracy mumbled, as if that said it all.

12.

"Are you nuts?"

The question struck Eric as funny so he laughed, his head thrown back, the .38 he'd taken from Blackjack stuffed into his waistband. The butt dug into his stomach as it jumped from his laughing, rubbing the skin underneath raw. He let it.

"I mean it, Eric," Tracy continued, easing herself to the floor of the Xerox room which Blackjack had turned over to them. It was one of the few actual rooms in the building with a real door that even locked from the inside. Eric locked it behind him. Blackjack had called this the settlement's honeymoon suite because its use was alternated every night by different couples. They had a sign-up sheet attached to a clipboard hanging on a nail outside the door.

"What's to think about, for Christ's sake," Tracy added. "Let's get our canoe and get the hell out of here."

Eric didn't answer her right away. He was thinking. Not about Blackjack's offer or Angel or Rhino or Alabaster or Liar's Cove. He was back to *The Centurion* and that woman he'd killed. Crow, they'd called her. She'd been singing outside their stateroom door.

"Every day, it's a gettin' closer, goin' faster than a roller coaster. . . ."

Eric backed against the long wooden table with its three-hole Hunt-Boston paper punch and green paper cutter still resting where it had before the quakes. He couldn't get that song out of his head.

"Love like yours will truly come my way. . . ."

He remembered Buddy Holly, his mom sneaking him into a concert when the Crickets played Tucson. Eric was nine. Everybody else's mother was always dragging him to hear Frankie Laine or Pat Boone. But Eric's mother liked to dance, to *move.* That night his father had remained on the Hopi reservation to haul a few more wheelbarrows of rocks from the mountain he was carving to resemble one of their legendary chiefs. His father didn't like Buddy Holly because of his black thick-rimmed glasses. "Makes him look like a busboy in an Oklahoma roadside diner."

"Come what may, do you ever long for true love from me-ee-ee?"

That was 1959. Three months later Buddy Holly died in a plane crash. Also on board was Ritchie Valens and J. P. Richardson. Eric's mother had cried, worn a black arm band while teaching her archeology class at the university that afternoon. At the end of class she played "Rave On" on a tinny old record player from the audiovisual department. That night Eric's father brought out his finest block of granite and started sculpting a bust of Buddy Holly for her. It took three years for him to finish and it was not very good because, though he was an enthusiastic artist, he was not very talented. But Eric's mother kept it on her piano long after Eric's father died.

Eric smiled at the memory, savoring it a bit. Good memories were so hard to recall these days, when one came he sometimes couldn't decide if it was of something that really had happened or if he was just making it up.

"Hey, earth to Eric. Come in, please." Tracy was waving at him.

"A little static, Houston Control. Can't copy."

She smiled. "Try an emergency landing, pal, 'cause Rod Serling has taken over down here. He's got us holed up in some flooded building that's been transformed into a farm. He's got us negotiating with some giant ex-pediatrician who claims he's a pirate, while avoiding an ape with a melted face and his companion, a Vietnamese Mata Hari with a kinky streak. And now—boy, Rod's really outdone himself this time—now he's got our heroes, Eric and Gimpy, discussing the possibility of kidnapping the aforementioned Vietnamese vixen

163

from under the nose of said custard-faced ape in the midst of some thieves' and murderers' hideout called Liar's Cove. California just ain't the mellow place it once was. On second thought, don't return to earth. Catch us on the rerun." She sighed, adjusting her hip for some comfort.

Eric laughed again, clapped his hands in appreciation. "I can't wait to read your book on this whole experience when we get off of here someday. A combination of Franz Kafka and Woody Allen."

"Well, I can't believe you actually told him we'd consider his scheme."

"Why not? It makes sense. We help out, in a purely advisory capacity, and get a free ride up to Santa Barbara on his ship. That alone will save us a lot of paddling. Think about your scabby little knees kneeling in that canoe for a few more days, paddling until your arms ache as if they'd been gnawed on by an alligator."

"Sweet talker."

"And with your hip, it'll be even worse. Plus we get as much fresh food as we want and the choice of weapons from the cache. There might be a few things there to help even the odds against Fallows and his bunch."

"I want to free Timmy, too, Eric, but—" Tracy started to protest when someone knocked on the door.

"Who is it?" she asked.

"Nurse Havczech. Got something for you."

Eric tilted the gun in his waistband for a fast

draw, then opened the door.

"Howdy," she said, walking into the room. With both hands she held a steaming mug which she offered to Tracy.

Tracy leaned forward to take it, smelling the steam as she leaned back again. She made a face. "Thanks, but what is it?"

"Don't ask, honey. It'll go down better that way."

Tracy sniffed it again, wrinkled her nose. "You sure I'm supposed to drink this and not use it to scrub the bathroom tiles?"

Nurse Havczech laughed as she turned to Eric. "She's quite a card, your lady."

"Keeps me in more stitches than an eight-inch knife wound."

Nurse Havczech stared dumbly at Eric. "That supposed to be funny?"

"Don't mind him," Tracy explained. "He's the ayatollah of comedy."

Nurse Havczech would have doubled over with laughter if her stomach hadn't been in the way. "You're a crack-up, lady. What my mom used to call 'the genuine article.'"

"It's nice to be appreciated," Tracy said, winking at Eric.

"Now you go and drink up that concoction, honey. Help you relax and get some sleep. Doctor sent it over."

"Blackjack?"

Nurse Havczech made a face at that name. "Yeah, that's what he calls himself."

Tracy frowned at the steaming mug.

"Now, don't fret. It's just a little distilled maple syrup made into a tea. We use it around here as an anesthetic."

Tracy looked at Eric, who shrugged. "Kind of a Mickey Finn," he said.

"Yeah, that's right, honey. Knock you on your ass for a few hours and give that hip of yours a chance to relax."

Tracy held her breath while she sipped the hot liquid. It slid across her tongue and down her throat with a soothing warmth. She took a breath. "Not too bad. Tastes a little like sweet and sour pork. I'm surprised he didn't send a few joints of grass along."

Nurse Havczech made a stern face like a mother defending her child. "Doctor might be a little bizarre, young lady, but he's still a damn fine medical man. He was one of the best in the state before this whole crazy mess and I won't hear anything bad about him."

"But just when his medical skills are most needed he's thrown them away to become a *pirate*."

Nurse Havczech sighed. "Peculiar, sure. But there's a lot about the situation you just don't know. Can't understand."

"Like what? Help me understand why a mature man with any ethics would do what he's done. Become what he's become."

"Can't," she said with a finality that left no doubt. She pressed her wrinkled lips together as if to demonstrate her inflexibility.

Eric lifted the only chair in the room, a gray

166

metal folding chair, and slid it next to Nurse Havczech. "How bad is his cancer?"

Nurse Havczech stared at Eric, and he could see the pain in her old watery eyes. She deflated a few inches with another heavy sign and sat down. "How'd you know?"

"Guessed. His baldness is a little patchy, like someone who's been through chemotherapy. And the marijuana. He didn't seem to enjoy it as a recreational treat. He seemed to need the relief."

"We grow some upstairs just for him. He'd never smoked before, so he's still getting used to it."

Tracy looked stunned. "That explains what he said before. That the quakes are the best thing that could have happened to him."

"Yeah, honey, that's the cynical way he's been since I've known him, but occasionally something else slips through. Something real fine. As a school nurse I'd had occasion to hear something bad about every pediatrician in Southern California. But I never did hear anything bad about Doctor."

"Then his whole pirate thing is just a game?"

"No, ma'am, not for a minute." She shook her head briskly. "He's one tough mother. He caught a couple of Rhino's crew once trying to sneak in here at night. A man and a woman 'bout your ages. He killed 'em both right on the spot. A regular execution. Nearly took the guy's head off with that saber of his. That thing's not just ornamental, you know." She looked at Eric.

"He's got a mean streak in him, a crazy urge to thumb his nose at the world. He's mad, goddamn it. Before the quakes he was being treated and there was some hope they'd be able to operate and clean him out. Save his life. But now . . ." She shrugged hopelessly. "Can you blame him for being what he is? He had a basketball scholarship to Temple University, was a cinch for the NBA. Got drafted in the lottery, sent to Vietnam in time to get a bullet through the ankle. Poof, no more basketball. Became a doctor instead. Then this cancer shit." She rubbed the bridge of her nose. "Told me once that as a kid he saw Mary Martin play Peter Pan on TV, and for two years after, all he used to dream of was being Peter Pan and going to Never-Never Land. Said he used to cry when he had to go to school because he wouldn't be able to think about Never-Never Land at school. Well," she smiled, "he finally got his wish, though Lord knows this is a poor substitute for Never-Never Land."

Nurse Havczech hoisted her plump body from the uncomfortable chair and shuffled toward the door. "Got to get back to my patients. We do quite a walk-in business there."

"Thanks for the tea, or whatever it is," Tracy called.

"Thank Dr. Blackjack," Nurse Havczech chuckled, shaking her head as she closed the door behind her.

"Quite a story," Tracy said, obviously impressed.

168

"Yeah," Eric nodded. "If it's true."

"God, you're cynical. Like him."

"Just cautious."

Tracy stretched out on the bedding, setting the mug on the floor near her head. It was no longer steaming. "We're going, aren't we? To Liar's Cove."

"That's not for me to decide alone. What do you think?"

"I think you still have a yen for the samurai sister."

"God, Tracy."

"Is it the danger? Knowing she carries a knife?" Tracy pulled the steel blade from her pocket. "Hell, I carried your arch support in my underwear. Can't get much more erotic than that."

Eric laughed. "The only feeling I have about Angel is regret that I didn't kill her back in 'Nam."

"What do you feel about me?"

"You already know."

Tracy lifted her eyes toward him, patted the blanket next to her. "Show me."

"Christ, Tracy, your hip."

"Show me."

Eric lifted the glass bell jar from the lantern and puffed out the tiny flame. The room winked into a grayish dark that still allowed them to see each other. Long, thin slivers of orange from the cracks in the door crisscrossed the dark like photo-sensor guards in clothing stores.

Eric tended to Tracy first, helping ease her out of the jeans and sweat shirt. He could see the pain wringing her face as she peeled the denim from around her hip wound, but there was no use in trying to talk any sense into her. She was like Annie that way. Once she decided something was important, there was no turning back. As she shifted on the pile of blankets, one of the rods of orange light flickered across her face like a sci-fi laser beam. It lit up the moisture in her eyes and he could see how important this was to her. Not just sex, but a ceremony. A bonding, an exchange of silent vows.

When she was finally naked, the white bandage taped to her hip in a lump like a jellyfish, Eric quickly shed his own clothing. He stretched out next to her. Carefully she rolled herself onto her good hip, exposing her back to him. She brought the knee of her leg up into a frozen ballet dancer's stance, only prone. Eric snuggled next to her, his body hair brushing against her smooth skin. He hung an arm over her stomach and was surprised at the hardness of the muscles there. It excited him, lifting his penis until it poked insistently against the back of her thigh.

She chuckled and began humming "Hail to the Chief."

"Jezz, how romantic," he said.

She didn't have to see him to know he was smiling. She wriggled her buttocks and back

170

closer, pressing herself flush against his solid body.

Eric let his hand brush lightly over her breast, swirling lazy circles like a child doodling in the sand. Feeling the nipples grow longer, harder. He thought about the crops growing upstairs, preferred the ones they were raising right here. He cupped her breast in his rough hand and massaged the nipple between thumb and forefinger, pinching harder and harder until he feared he might be hurting her, knowing he wasn't. Her breathing was shallow now, a husky panting.

She reached behind her, groped for his penis, finally snagging it with a firm grasp. She squeezed and he could feel her callouses and blisters pricking his tender skin. It made him harder, hungrier. Still, he was cautious.

"I'm wounded, Eric, not dead," she said. "We can do the slow gentle bit later. Right now, I just want to get laid."

He smiled, dipped his head over her shoulder to kiss her. Their eyes were open, staring deep into each other's as their tongues bumped like playful dolphins. The orange light sizzled along Eric's scar and she squeezed him harder, using her other hand to crush his hand tighter over her breast.

"God, Eric, it's been so long."

He understood. The mechanics of sex were much different in this California than they had been before. No more birth-control pills. Prophylactics were rare anymore. Those that cared, reverted to the rhythm method, the only one that didn't require any devices. Big Bill Tenderwolf had once told him about using stoneseed roots to suppress the estrous cycle, but Big Bill had preferred a vasectomy. Eric could have had a vasectomy done at University Camp when they were being encouraged, but he'd seen no need to since Annie was no longer able to give birth after Timmy. Now he was glad he hadn't. What if anything should happen to Timmy? Would he ever want to start over again with another family? With Tracy?

It made him guilty to even think such thoughts. As long as Timmy was alive, that was all that mattered.

He skated his hand over her buttocks, nestling between her legs into her soft pubic hairs. They were matted, wet and sticky, and he calculated how long since they'd last made love. Two weeks, three. They'd run out of rubbers, the little boxes of Trojans they'd carried in their backpack along with other necessities of life. He hadn't used one since and that made him feel like a high school student, fumbly and sweaty. When they'd run out, Tracy had just passed her menstrual cycle. She was within days of her period; he could relax.

Tracy lifted her leg slightly, guiding his engorged penis to her. The head bumped, then skidded along the slippery path, disappearing.

Their movements were smooth, less energetic than usual in deference to Tracy's wound. But there was something almost more passionate about this, a sense of ritual that touched both of them. He could feel the filmy sweat bristling over her skin as they rocked together. Her eyelids fluttered as usual, her mouth wide open and sucking air. Morbidly it reminded him of when she was drowning earlier. Then all the air rushed out of her lungs and she clenched her teeth. He felt her vaginal muscles rippling like a strong tide along his penis. He hurried a few more strokes, tensed his buttocks, and gushed bubbling lava into her.

They hugged without words for a while. He watched her eyes close, her face relax into sleep. Her lips puffed loosely. Watching her in the dark, he realized something he'd avoided accepting for too long. "I love you," he whispered.

She opened her eyes and turned to face him. "Gotcha." She smiled.

He smiled back, pulled a ragged blanket over them.

Book Three:

LIAR'S COVE

Let me have the fire. The first thing is to purify the place.

—Homer

13.

"How's the hip?"

Tracy looked up from *The Argo*'s railing where she'd been leaning, watching the water foam and boil against the slick hull. "Hi, Blackjack."

"Hi yourself. Getting plenty of rest?"

"Too much. I'm antsy."

He smiled. "Good sign. Just don't try to overdo it."

"Considering where we're going and what we're going to do when we get there, that's kinda dumb advice, wouldn't you say?"

He laughed, his mouth wide and his dark eyes twinkling. "Yeah, I guess so. Where's your partner in crime?"

"Eric? He's sitting over there, on the other side of that sail. See him?"

Blackjack cupped his hands around his eyes like binoculars, shading them from the brisk wind and glare of the sun. "Right.

What's he doing?''

"Thinking, I guess.''

"He's a tough man,'' Blackjack said, admiration tinting the words.

"He's a good man,'' Tracy corrected. "There's a difference.''

"Well, let's go interrupt his meditation and discuss the dull business of kidnapping.''

Tracy limped across the deck using the special cane Eric had fashioned for her out of the remains of that Piper Cub. It clomped on the deck of the ship as she walked after Blackjack, and it made her feel a little like Captain Ahab pacing with his peg leg, raking the ocean for Moby Dick. Her hip still alternated between dull throb and sharp ache, but both seemed to be lessening significantly. She could even run now. More painful was the knowledge that she would walk with this slight limp for the rest of her life. What disturbed her the most wasn't so much the fact of the limp, but that it was a flaw that she could never improve. It wasn't like dry hair or oily skin or chubby thighs or bad posture. All of them defects that had plagued her at one time in her adolescence, all of which she'd overcome. The only thing that had helped her live with it so far was Eric's support. He helped her without pampering her. Didn't give her the chance to feel sorry for herself. Sometimes he even called her Peggy, short for peg leg. Others on board thought him cruel, but it made her laugh.

"How do you like our colors, Ravensmith?''

Blackjack asked.

Eric was sitting cross-legged on the deck, wrapping something around his wrist. He glanced up at the flag being hoisted up. Skull and crossbones. "Catchy."

"Great, huh? I bought it at Liar's Cove. Somebody had taken it from Disneyland."

"What's that, Eric?" Tracy asked, pointing at his wrist.

He quickly unwrapped the leather thongs attached to a small leather patch and held it up. "A slingshot. I stripped the leather from one of those executive chairs back at the farm settlement." He started rewrapping it around his wrist, knotting the end with one hand and his teeth. When he was finished it looked like a crude leather watchband. "This way even if they take my bow, I'll still have something."

"Nice," Blackjack approved. "That's just the kind of soldier's thinking we hired you for."

Eric looked up at him. "I heard you were a soldier too. In 'Nam."

"Nope," Blackjack shook his head vigorously. "I was there, but never any kind of a soldier. I was a C.O."

"A C.O.?" Tracy asked.

"Conscientious objector. It wasn't a dodge, either. I really was morally opposed to any kind of violence. I'd had enough as the only black kid in a fancy white neighborhood in Philly. Only my draft board didn't see it that way. It didn't compute that a nigger wouldn't take to fighting like he would to dancing. So, like magic I was transformed from a promising basketball player to a medic."

"What happened to that conscientious objector?" Eric asked, looking up at the skull-and-crossbones flag flapping overhead.

Blackjack laughed bitterly. "The kid's grown up."

"Has he?" Eric stood up, stared across the bow of the ship at the wedge of land on the horizon. "That it?"

"Yup, that's Liar's Cove."

Eric turned his head to face Blackjack, his reddish-brown eyes glowing. "That can't be Liar's Cove."

"Afraid so," he smiled.

Tracy squinted toward the horizon as the land grew larger, clearer. She looked confused. "You know what that looks like?"

"Yes," Eric said. "Hearst Castle."

14.

"Like hell!" Blackjack barked, grabbing Eric's shoulder and shoving him sharply.

Eric stumbled backward a few steps on the wet deck before regaining his balance. His shoulder tingled where Blackjack had grabbed him. The strength in the man startled Eric. "That's the way it's going to be. Get used to the idea."

"You're nuts. I'm not leaving my whole crew on the ship while the three of us go waltzing in there alone."

"It's the only way. From what you've described, there are at least a couple hundred permanent residents here, and a couple hundred others visiting for business or pleasure. Even with the ten other crew members you've got we're hopelessly out-numbered. But as just three people, they won't consider us much of a threat. We'll have a chance."

Blackjack massaged his temples, his face

pinched together as if fighting a migraine headache. "This is where Lee Marvin says, 'Maybe one man can get behind enemy lines and do the job a whole army couldn't.'" His eyes blazed with pain and anger.

"No, this is where you let me do what I agreed to do. Kidnap Angel."

Blackjack sprinkled some marijuana on a Zig-Zag paper, rolled, licked, and lit it. He tossed the book of matches to Eric. "From Rachel's collection. She used to take them from every restaurant and hotel she and her husband visited. She has a gallon jar filled with them. It's the only thing she saved from their house when it was destroyed. Can you imagine that?"

It was a rhetorical question, so Eric didn't answer. He knew what was going through Blackjack's mind. Despite her pleading and arguments, Rachel had been left behind to continue directing the farm. Eric had noticed the relief on Blackjack's face when she'd finally agreed not to come along.

Eric read the matchbook cover—Reuben E. Lee Restaurant and Cocktail Lounge—and tossed it back to Blackjack.

Blackjack sucked in a cloud of smoke. "Sorry about the misunderstanding. You're the boss right now. That's what I'm paying you for, right?" He spread a cool, lazy smile across his face.

"Right."

The two men stood side by side next to the railing and watched the ship swerve toward shore. Tracy exhaled a long breath of relief, relaxing the stiff fingers tensed around her cane. She had to admit that she didn't much like Eric's three-against-the-world plan either, but she knew enough to trust him. Still, with the two of them fighting, this little mission was going to be even more difficult.

"The whole place used to be on a sixteen hundred-foot hill, five miles from beach to castle. But now . . ." He shrugged. The ocean had swallowed most of what once was a hill. Lapping only a few hundred feet away from the buildings, the water swirled and paced, as if waiting hungrily for the rest of the shore.

Five clumsily constructed docks floating on oil drums spread out into the water like a bony hand, far enough to allow ships to tie up without anchoring out to sea.

"That's awfully nice of them to have built this," Tracy said, as Blackjack helped her over the side onto the dock.

"They don't do anything around here to be nice. It's here to bring in customers. Period."

Eric slipped the compound bow over his shoulder, adjusting the quiver of arrows on his hip. It wasn't as nice as his old bow, but it would do.

Blackjack gave a few last-minute instructions to his crew, then vaulted over the railing, his saber jangling against his leg. "Let's go have some fun, shall we?"

They wrangled their way through the crowded docks bustling with people loading and unloading cargo from their ships. Some brought bound women, hefting a woman over one shoulder and a sack of grain over the other. Two sailors wrestled with a reluctant cow that refused to walk down the gangplank, pausing instead to relieve its bowels.

There was no consistent fashion as to what people wore. Men and women alike wore the uniforms of scavengers, mismatched scraps of whatever they could find. A suede jacket, once worth eight hundred dollars, was worn over a too-large polyester shirt that had brought in $8.99 to J. C. Penney. The one consistent item they all wore was a weapon, their hands never straying too far from the butts of revolvers, the hilts of knives. All eyes were at once suspicious, fearful, predatory.

The ships that crowded the docks were of all sizes and shapes. Rowboats hugged against schooners, catamarans nosed between yachts. Some boats were homemade hybrids, designed to accommodate whatever materials were on hand, with homemade sails fashioned from tarps stitched together.

The dock bounced and swayed in the water as Tracy, Eric, and Blackjack nudged their way through the bustling people. Occasionally someone would fall off the side of the dock, into the water or onto a ship, but people acted as if that was to be expected. One man elbowed past Tracy, each hand gripped tightly around the throat of two squawking chickens. A cloud of feathers from their flapping wings puffed into her face and made her sneeze.

"There," Tracy said, waving the feathers away with one hand and scratching her nose with the other. "Over there on the first dock."

Eric and Blackjack followed her nod. Icicles sprouted in their stomachs at the recognition. There was no mistaking the ship lashed alongside the first dock.

The Centurion.

"It's like something out of *Ali Baba and the Forty Thieves*," Tracy said in wonderment as she looked around.

"It is amazing," Blackjack agreed, "no matter how many times you come here."

"God, it's like those bazaars in Marrakech or somewhere. You expect to see snake handlers any second now."

Eric didn't say anything. He watched; he studied. Tracy was right, though. Whatever Hearst Castle looked like before the quake, it had since been transformed into a giant marketplace crowded with jostling, sweating, dirty people, each with something to buy, sell, or trade.

"This is the courtyard of Casa Grande," Blackjack explained. "Casa Grande's that big four-story mother there. That's where old William Randolph used to hump Marion Davies, when he wasn't having Clark Gable over for the weekend." He pointed to various areas beyond the building. "Over on the other

185

side are a few more mansions. One's a whore-house now, the other two are kinda like hotels. That's where Rhino and Angel will be staying while they're here."

Tracy nodded. "Casa del Sol, Casa del Monte, and, uh, Casa del something. Oh yeah, Casa del Mar. They were all built as guesthouses."

Eric turned to look at her. "I didn't know you were a Hearst Castle buff."

"I'm not. I'm court artist, remember? I got my start with Patty Hearst's trial when they shot up that sporting goods store. I used to sit in that courtroom and sketch her, thinking how, except for a couple hundred million dollars, there wasn't much difference between us. A couple of Homecoming Queen–types trying to . . . I don't know . . . *matter.*" She glanced off into the lush green hills surrounding them. "Anyway, I've been here a dozen times to study the art works. The place is a kaleidoscope of art treasures."

"Yeah, well, when the present occupants are done, it'll be a kaleidoscope of junk."

Street vendors were shouting at passers-by, hawking their wares with a festive enthusiasm. *"Am-mu-ni-tion!"* one bald man with a black mustache shouted. "We make ammo for almost any gun. C'mon in here and check us out." A line of people with various guns formed around the open-air booth. It was like a carnival, Eric thought, remembering the last one he'd been to. A Fireman's Fish Fry and Carnival. The kids ate corn dogs, then insisted on immediately riding the Twister. Afterward the corn dogs were deposited on the grass in a mushy heap.

While the bald man gathered potential customers, a teenaged version of the man hunched over a Corbin Swaging Press, turning a .22 Long Rifle case into a .224-caliber bullet for a woman in a red hunting cap clutching a Mini-14. A spool of copper refrigeration tubing was coiled on the ground next to the press, soon to be turned into bullet casings.

Next door to him a fat woman in a cowboy hat was gluing feathers to shafts, while an even fatter woman fastened nocks onto the ends of the arrows. "We got arrows," she barked to no one in particular. "Reasonable prices." She saw Eric looking at her and spoke directly to him. "Fletching is real turkey feathers, mister."

Eric inspected the feathers, tossed them back down on the table. "Pigeons."

She threw her hands up and cackled out a laugh that had people turning to see what the noise was. "Pigeons is right," she said, and cackled again.

Next door to this booth was a shoe repair shop. An old man with quivering hands and a kindly face did his best to patch up shoes and sneakers. Some customers he turned away, unable to help, always giving them a sad smile of apology. Eric noticed the faded blue numbers tattooed on the underside of his wrist and felt a sharp pang of humility. Here was a man who had survived the concentration camps of Germany and who was surviving still, offering good humor to those around him. Of all the sights he'd seen so far in Liar's Cove, this one impressed him the most.

"Those guys with the Hearst Castle T-shirts," Blackjack said, tugging on Eric's sleeve, "those are the security force around here. They'll know Rhino and his gang and probably can tell us where to find them." He walked over to one of the security force, a skinny kid with a .22 Hi-Standard Durango revolver sticking out of the pocket of his corduroy pants. He wore a white T-shirt with an image of Hearst Castle on it and five stripes of dirt across the chest where he'd wiped his fingers. He was talking to a young girl, no older than fifteen, who wore a thin steak knife in her belt. Eric watched Blackjack talk to the kid, who grudgingly answered, anxious to brush the black man off so he could get back to the girl. But Blackjack wouldn't be brushed off. He kept smiling and talking, leaning his six feet four inches over the kid until he got what he wanted.

"Bad news," he said, when he returned.

"Is there any other kind around here?" Tracy asked.

"Rhino and Angel are in the Main Vestibule."

Eric shrugged. "So?"

"So, that's where the guy who runs Liar's Cove is. The guy I was hoping we'd be able to avoid. You see all this scum around here?" He swept his hand in a wide arc. "Well, multiply it by a hundred and you get a feel for the moral

188

level of BeBop."

"BeBop?" Tracy laughed. "What's a BeBop?"

"BeBop is the dude who decides who lives and dies in here. And his word is final."

Eric started off toward the entrance to Casa Grande. "I guess it's time we met him. And he met us."

15.

Howling laughter rumbled through the building as they squeezed their way through the rowdy crush of bodies. Most of the people in Casa Grande were slurping from metal cups.

"What are they drinking?" Tracy asked Blackjack. "Smells like gasoline."

"Close," Blackjack said. "A home-brew that BeBop cooks up himself. I once saw him drink a quart of it, then pour the rest into an empty motorcycle and drive it around the courtyard. I wouldn't give two cents for any of their livers a year from now."

A drunken woman wearing a Padres' baseball cap leaned over Tracy's shoulder and laughed. "Man, who cares what happens a year from now." She drained the contents of her cup and sprayed it through her lips straight up into the air. It rained back down in her face and she laughed again before disappearing into the boiling crowd.

"This is a little like some fraternity parties I've attended," Tracy said. A stricken look crumpled her face. "Oh no. Look at that." She pointed to a couple standing by an ornate doorway. The man was carving a big heart in the column with his knife. The girl giggled coyly, flipping a curtain of long, greasy hair over her shoulder. "Jesus, stop him. That doorway is solid marble, created by Andrea Sansovino, a sixteenth-century Florentine sculptor." They watched as the man continued to jab his knife at the marble, chipping and scratching his crude heart with wobbly initials.

"It's too late to try to save this place," Eric said softly.

"Yeah, you're right," she said, forcing a smile. "But I'll bet you're impressed by what *I* know for a change, huh?"

"*I* am," Blackjack said.

Eric winked at her and she smiled broadly as she limped ahead, pleased. The information wasn't medicine or survival, just the most useless of fields in this crazy world: art. But still, it was all hers. Something she knew that they didn't. Something she could be proud of.

As they pushed their way closer to the Main Vestibule, the pounding beat of music wafted to them.

"Somebody's beating that guitar within an inch of its life," Blackjack said.

"Do you play?" Tracy asked him, shouting to be heard above the noise.

"I know three chords. Enough to play twenty-three verses of 'Louie, Louie.'"

"That sounds like two more chords than whoever's playing knows," Eric said.

Finally they wedged through the arms and legs of the multipede blob of stinking bodies into the Main Vestibule. Standing in front of a magnificently carved fireplace mantel, his leg up on a squat black table, stood a bony man of about thirty. He wore a poncho made from a large American flag, a slit cut in the middle for his head, the field of stars flapping against his blue-jeaned shins. His feet were bare. He was whacking the guitar with broad strokes, singing loudly, a mouthful of braces reflecting light.

"I don't care what people say, rock 'n' roll is here to stay." Behind him a kid about thirteen banged on a set of drums in a haphazard rhythm that ignored the song they were both singing.

"That's BeBop on guitar," Blackjack explained. "The kid on the drums is his, uh, protégé. Calls him Tsetse, like the fly."

Eric nodded, then directed their attention to the corner of the room, where Rhino and Angel were standing, flanked on all sides by some of their crew from *The Centurion*. A couple of crew members were slurping from metal cups. Rhino tugged restlessly on the rubber band around his wrist. Angel watched BeBop's performance with piercing eyes, like a chef studying a pheasant it was about to carve. It was the only look she had.

Abruptly, BeBop stopped hammering the guitar and waved a hand at the drummer to stop too. Everyone applauded dutifully, whistling and yelling. BeBop took a deep bow, turned his back to the crowd a moment, flipped up his poncho, and began pissing into the fireplace.

Tracy shook her head. "That sixteen-foot high fireplace he's pissing into is from the French Renaissance. The marble busts surmounting it are by, uh . . ."

"François Duquesnoy," Eric finished.

She looked up at him, trying not to show her annoyance. "Figures. It goddamn figures."

He slipped an arm around her waist and felt her lean into him, shifting weight from her bad hip. She felt good there.

When BeBop had finished zipping his pants and turned around, everyone applauded again even louder. He flashed his mouthful of braces.

"Hey, lookie, lookie," he said, pointing over the heads of the crowd. "It's my old buddy, Black Jack."

"That's Blackjack, man. One word, like the card game."

"Right, man. I didn't mean anything of a racist nature by it. After all, you're the guy who helped me concoct my world famous BeBop's Brew." He hoisted a metal cup and took a deep swig. Everyone cheered and did the same.

Eric and Tracy turned curious eyes on Blackjack, who shrugged. "A little medicinal consultation. For a fee, of course."

"Of course," Eric said.

"What'd you come for this time?" BeBop asked. "Buying or selling?"

"A little bit of both, maybe. Brought some customers."

"Well, bring 'em on out here where I can get a look at them."

Eric and Tracy stepped away from the crowd. Blackjack hovered behind them, his hand resting idly on the hilt of his saber.

"Who are you?" BeBop asked, his pale blue eyes out of place in his dark-featured face.

Blackjack answered for them. "Eric Ravensmith and Tracy Ammes. They're with my crew now," he said, turning to face the whole crowd, "so I don't want anybody to try to cheat them."

"Ravensmith, huh?" BeBop said. "I've heard something about you. Can't remember what."

"Savvytown," Rhino said from his corner. His face was contorted with anger, his one black eye shimmering under the overhang of twisted flesh.

"Right, right. You're the dude that went in there and smashed the joint up. Yeah, I remember now. Slick piece of work. You don't plan to try that here, do you?" BeBop was grinning around his braces, but the cold look in his eyes was unmistakable.

"No," Eric assured him. "That was personal."

"Okay, then let me lay out the rules here at Liar's Cove. They're my rules and they aren't up for negotiation. You follow them, fine. You break them, you're dead. No exceptions. With me so far?"

"Go on."

"Any business transaction that takes place anywhere on the premises is taxable. That means I get ten percent for providing the place. You can only buy food here from my kitchen. You can stay at my hotel over at Casa del Mar or you can visit my whorehouse at Casa del Sol. We got men, women, children, or any combination you can think of. And before you get the wrong idea, I don't run them. They rent the rooms from me and give a percentage. Nobody's forcing them to do anything. They want to leave, they can walk out of here today." He grinned, his mouth twinkling metal. "Hell, I've got a fucking waiting list over there anyway. That should give you plenty of room to conduct whatever business you came here for. My security force is here to keep the violence at a minimum. I don't make any money if you people end up killing each other, so unnecessary violence will not be tolerated. You have to think of this place as a new concept in the shopping mall. The only restriction is in this building, Casa Grande." He gestured grandly as if to encompass the whole building. "It's got some one hundred rooms, including basements, vaults, thirty-seven bedrooms, and forty-one bathrooms. Put the whole thing together and you got seventy-three thousand five hundred ten square feet, almost one and a half times the size of a football field. And it's all mine. Other than the first floor, the rest of this house is off limits, man. This is where I do my Orson Welles impression. Dig?"

Eric nodded.

"Too bad my mom couldn't be around to see me now," he said, addressing the crowd. He'd gotten used to speaking to large groups and seemed to prefer it rather than one-on-one conversations. "After all, it's thanks to her I'm here. She used to be head tour guide here for years." He pointed at the Hearst Castle T-shirt one of his security guards was wearing. "We had five boxes of those T-shirts in our garage. Factory seconds the gift shop couldn't sell. We had a Hearst Castle clock in the living room, Hearst Castle dishes in the kitchen." He sat on the edge of the squat black table, absently strumming the guitar. "This place supported both of us while I played soft rock in Holiday Inns on weekends. John Denver shit. 'Play "Rocky Mountain High,"' written in lipstick on cocktail napkins with a dollar bill attached. Same old shit." He leaned the guitar against the table, waved the young drummer over. "Bring the medicine bag, Kid," he said.

The young boy grabbed a child's lunch

bucket with cartoon figures of Donnie and Marie Osmond painted on the lid. In his other hand he carried a thin pole. He wore a fisherman's hat that was stuck through with dozens of what looked like hat pins. He handed the lunch pail to BeBop, who opened it, dabbed some white powder on the tip of his thumbnail, and snorted it up his nostril. Then he closed the pail and handed it back. He turned to Eric with a crooked grin. "Hey, Ravensmith, you or your chick wouldn't happen to be a dentist, would you? I can't seem to get these damn braces off."

"Sorry, can't help you," Eric said.

"Well, that's what I get, trying to straighten my teeth at my age. Show business, you know?"

"Listen, BeBop," Rhino suddenly said, stomping forward from his group. Angel tried to stop him, but he shrugged her off.

Eric saw Griffin follow Rhino forward; he was carrying Eric's crossbow.

Rhino shook a delicate finger at BeBop. "I want this Ravensmith and Blackjack. They've caused me considerable business setbacks."

"How so?" BeBop asked.

"Well, they tried to destroy my ship, killed several of my crew."

BeBop smiled. "Since that forced you to come here for supplies and repairs and to recruit more crew members, they actually did me a favor. I'm turning a profit on the deal."

"I don't give a damn about your profit,"

Rhino bellowed, snapping the rubber band against his thick wrist. "I want them. So if it's profit you want, I'll buy them from you."

BeBop arched his eyebrows in surprise. "Now there's an offer I haven't had before. Pirates *buying* other pirates. What should I say to that, Ravensmith?"

Eric smiled. "I'd ask him how much he's offering."

BeBop laughed and the crowd joined in, toasting Eric. "Okay, then, Rhino, what's your offer. How much for the three of them?"

"I'll give you their ship and all its contents."

"I could take that myself if I wanted to. But then how many customers would come here to do business if they didn't feel safe. No, Rhino, I'm afraid whatever conflict you have with the doctor and his friends will have to wait until you leave Liar's Cove."

"I want him!" Rhino yelled, his lumpish body trembling with energy and rage.

One of Rhino's crew snatched an arrow up and laid it into his bow, pivoting toward Eric.

BeBop nodded at his young sidekick, who immediately plucked one of the hat pins from his fishing cap, thumbed it into the end of the hollow tube he was carrying, pointed it at Rhino's man, and blew sharply into the end. The hat pin launched out of the end of the tube and dove into the neck of the crewman. The man dropped his bow with a howl and grabbed his neck. Blood braided down his throat as he swooned to the floor.

The crowd watched silently.

"I warned you that violence wouldn't be tolerated. It's bad for business. Nothing personal, Rhino."

Angel quickly nudged Rhino's elbow, guiding him through the crowd. "Of course we understand," she said politely. "We apologize for our friend's rashness."

"No problem," BeBop said. "Tsetse needed the practice anyway."

Angel led Rhino out of the room, stepping over the twitching body of their wounded crew member. Kelly Furst, the black ex-army nurse, and Rilke stopped to pick up their fallen comrade.

"I wouldn't bother," BeBop smiled. "Tsetse dips those suckers in something nasty that Blackjack helped him cook up. That guy'll be dead meat in a couple minutes. We can use the body to feed the hogs."

Kelly Furst and Rilke exchanged looks, dropped the body, and quickly trotted after the others.

When they were gone and the crowd was loudly discussing the events just past, BeBop waved Eric, Tracy, and Blackjack over. "That Rhino's getting worse and worse, man. Acts like a junkie speed freak on Angel Dust. I don't know what your beef is, but I know he's out for your asses. Personally, I don't care one way or the other who does what to who, but I don't want it done here. You know the rules, folks. I'd hate to end up feeding you guys to the hogs too. Blackjack and me done too much business together for that." He paused, let the light flicker off his braces. "And he knows me well enough to know I'll kill all three of you if I have to."

16.

"It's like Times Square," Tracy complained. "Don't they ever go to bed around here?"

"They save that for Casa del Sol," Blackjack said. "There you can buy a bed and some company in it for anywhere between a loaded cartridge and a bunch of fresh spinach."

They were walking casually through the lower lobby of Casa del Mar, picking their way past the endless throngs of people. Around them loomed the ancient artworks of centuries past. The ceilings, pilasters, and doorways were gilt decorated. On the wall near the heavy wooden hand-carved door was a polychrome stucco relief of the Madonna and Child by Mino da Fiesole, a fifteenth-century Florentine sculptor. Pushed against one wall was a gilt wood, marble-topped eighteenth-century table from Italy. A couple of rough-hewn men were snoring in a drunken stupor on top of the table, their heavy boots having already scraped long furrows of gilt from the legs.

"Don't you think we should go back and get the rest of my crew?" Blackjack asked. "I mean, now that Rhino knows we're here, they're sure to be extra cautious."

"What for? They don't know why we're here. Rhino doesn't know that Angel double-crossed him with Alabaster. And Angel doesn't know that we know. If anything, they'll be out looking for us, afraid that we've already turned tail and run." Eric glanced up at Blackjack. "As long as the information you bought is accurate, we should be in pretty good shape."

"The information is good. Like the newspapers used to say, 'a reliable source.' Actually I got it from one of BeBop's security people. He doesn't discourage them from accepting bribes as long as it doesn't interfere with his percentage. He has a very pragmatic philosophy."

"He's nuts," Tracy said.

"Yes," Blackjack agreed. "There is that too."

"Okay, we know this place is so crowded they had to put Rhino and his people all on different floors. Angel's room is on the third floor, Rhino's is on the first, and in between, Griffin and the rest of the crew are sharing a room on the second floor. That spreads them out adequately for our purposes. It's too bad they couldn't split them up and send a few over to Casa del Monte, but this arrangement will have to do."

As they walked up the wooden stairs, Eric couldn't help but marvel at his surroundings.

Even in the shambles these animals were making of it, the building's regal beauty was dominating. Hearst had been possessed when he'd built it, overseeing every detail with architect Julia Morgan, from imported tiles to bathroom fixtures. A massive construction job that contributed to the $125,000,000 debt that eventually destroyed Hearst. The bitter irony: four years before his death, his bad heart forced him to leave his Enchanted Hill to be nearer medical attention.

It was his fantasy, Eric thought, like Blackjack's fantasy of becoming a pirate. Now in California anyone could live out their fantasies; anyone could be a William Randolph Hearst. BeBop could go from part-time musician to ruler of a feudal city-state. Apparently no one had learned from Hearst's mistakes. Without controls, fantasies are closer to nightmares than dreams.

When they reached the third floor, they picked their way cautiously past the people sleeping in the hallway or haggling over a deal or telling raunchy jokes over a Mason jar of BeBop's Brew. It looked like the corridors of a Las Vegas hotel during a Teamsters' convention.

"Recognize anybody?" Eric asked.

Tracy shook her head. "I don't remember them from *The Centurion.*"

"Me neither," Blackjack said.

"Okay, let's do it. As long as they aren't around, this shouldn't be too difficult."

Eric gripped his bow with one hand, the arrow already nocked into place, and cupped his other hand around the door knob to Angel's room. He rocked backward as if to smash his shoulder into the door. Blackjack laid a restraining hand on his shoulder. "The locks have been removed," he whispered. "BeBop's house rules."

Eric pushed the door open.

"Come on," Rhino snapped at Griffin. "Grab your new toy and let's go."

Griffin hefted Eric's Barnett Commando crossbow from his bed and leaned it against his shoulder. There were only two beds in the room, one a sixteenth-century fourposter, the other a copy. Griffin had one, the Peterson brothers shared the other. The rest of the crew flopped out on the floor.

"What's up, Cap?" Griffin said a little too loudly. He'd had too much of BeBop's Brew, but didn't want Rhino to know.

"I want you and a few of the others to go upstairs and escort Angel down to my room."

"Can do, Cap," Griffin said, but moaned to himself. That bitch would put up a fight about it. Oh, she'd come all right—no one refused a request by Rhino—but she'd make them all miserable the whole way down. And his head was already throbbing from the booze. He stuffed a few bolts for the crossbow in his belt. "Kelly, Danton," he pointed, snapping his fingers at them, "you come with me."

Kelly Furst was naked, sitting cross-legged on her blanket reading a year-old issue of *Cosmopolitan* she'd bought from a vendor in the courtyard. He'd wanted her to come to his room that night, but had settled for a hand job, which she'd performed right there in his booth in the middle of the flowing crowd. She'd opened his fly, reached in, and nodded. No one paid any attention while he thrust his skinny pelvis against her hand. It hadn't taken long. She took a copy of *Redbook* too, which wasn't part of the bargain, but he didn't bother arguing with her.

She bent the corner of the page to mark her place in the article entitled "Barspeak: The Art of Conversation at Singles Bars," stood up, pulled on her shorts and sleeveless T-shirt, and grabbed her bow.

Richard Danton did ten rapid-fire pushups before leaping to his feet with a crooked grin. At eighteen, he was always ready for something to do. He was one of the new recruits they'd just taken on today and he was looking forward to proving himself. The biggest shock in young Danton's life so far hadn't been the quakes or the subsequent death of his parents, but the fact that he didn't feel bad when he killed people. The discovery that his parents had been all wrong about that had set him free. He'd killed twelve people since, each represented by a notch on the handle of the axe he carried.

"I want her in my room in five minutes,"

Rhino said, pacing. In the past couple of days he'd lost the ability to stand still at all. His body *had* to keep moving, constantly rocking, pacing, fidgeting. Even inside he felt like everything was moving, the organs vibrating, shifting uncomfortably, jockeying against each other for a more comfortable position. If you stopped and thought about it, you could go crazy. . . .

"We'll be back faster than a cat can bury his shit," Griffin said, cocking the crossbow and sliding a bolt into the groove. Kelly and Danton followed him out, their weapons clutched at their chests, ready.

Angel was already moving.

Wearing only blue panties and a white sweat shirt, she did a handspring over the bed, somersaulting lightly onto her feet next to her pile of weapons. Her hand passed over the pile and suddenly she was holding a stack of sharpened throwing stars.

Eric and Blackjack flanked toward her in separate arcs, like a wishbone. Eric held the bow string taut, but didn't yet draw it back. Blackjack drew his saber, holding the hilt with both hands like a Jimmy Connors backhand. Tracy leaned against the closed door, guarding it with her thick cane.

Angel's eyes darted back and forth among the three of them, her back slightly arched. Eric could see her mind flipping through strategies, countermoves, options, like a Go player rubbing a black stone before making the winning move. When her eyes finally settled on Tracy, he knew she planned to go straight for the door.

"Duck, Trace," Eric shouted, echoing his plea from a couple days ago when they were still happily on their canoe.

Only this time she didn't argue. Tracy twisted away from the door just as Angel's wrist snapped, flicking a spinning star across the room like a tiny buzz-saw blade gone berserk. The star thudded into the oak door, splintering the carved face of an English hunter chasing a fox. A second star followed almost immediately, this one pinning a lock of Tracy's hair to the door. The metal points fanned out just two inches from her left eye.

"Enough, Angel," Eric said, drawing the bow string back to his cheek. The tip of the arrow quivered slightly as it pointed at her small body.

Angel's smile was faint. A dare, he thought. She had more confidence in her perfect body's agility than she did fear of Eric's arrow. Suddenly she grabbed the ragged blanket from the bed and flipped it into the air toward Eric. He'd hesitated, not wanting to kill her until she'd reproduced Alabaster's map, but the ghosting blanket startled him into releasing his grip. The arrow plunged into the blanket like a missile, pulling the whole thing high over their heads, finally nailing the blanket to the wall.

But Angel had already cartwheeled over the bed, bouncing to her feet in time to fling two more stars. The first took a glancing bite out of Eric's thigh, chewing off a hunk of denim and skin before dropping tiredly to the floor. The second plunked below Blackjack's collarbone, lodging between bones.

"Damn," he yelled, more from anger than pain, struggling to pluck it out of his body. It wouldn't give.

Angel's hand found the door knob.

Whoomp!

Tracy whirled around with her cane and smacked Angel in the lower spine. She was off balance because of her hip, so she wasn't able to put much power behind the blow. But the effort yanked her hair free, leaving a lock of her hair still stuck to the door under the throwing star.

Angel's body arced backward from the impact. She dropped to the floor, her hands still clutching the door knob. Weakly she tried to pull herself back up. Too late. Eric grabbed a handful of her long black hair and jerked her backward onto the floor.

Blackjack pressed the saber against the hollow of her throat, denting the skin slightly.

"At last, Eric, you have come to finish your assignment of so long ago." Tears of pain spilled from Angel's eyes, but otherwise she showed no emotion.

"That was another planet, another man," Eric said, kneeling beside her.

"Yes," she said, squinting into his eyes, studying him. "You are changed. I see something of our old friend in you now. Something

210

dark behind the eyes. A tint of Fallows, perhaps." She smiled. "He bragged to me that he would turn you or kill you. I see he has succeeded."

Eric smiled. "If that's true, Angel, you have much to fear from me. *N'est-ce pas?*"

"Out of the way, asshole," Griffin said, shoving the large drunk out of his way. The big man bounced into the wall, scraping his nose on the Italian Renaissance tempura-on-wood painting. In his stupor, he thought the woman in the painting resembled Betty, his ex-wife, as he furiously snatched it from the wall and spun around to clobber Griffin with it. Griffin swung the heavy metal butt of the crossbow around, clipping the drunk on the temple. The skin didn't break, but a discolored splotch of blood pooled into a dark full moon on his forehead as he sank to the floor, unconscious. Kelly Furst stepped over the body as if nothing had happened. Richard Danton kicked the unconscious man in the crotch as he passed by and giggled.

Few in the crowded corridor seemed to notice. And those that did notice, didn't care.

Somebody reached out and touched Kelly's dreadlocks as she walked by. White people were always doing that, so she ignored it and kept walking.

When they finally bullied their way to Angel's door, Griffin took a deep breath, rolled his eyes in expectation, and knocked.

There was a pause, so he knocked again, using the butt of the crossbow. A chip of carved wood with a fox's tail flew off.

"Who is it?" Angel asked.

"Benny and the Jets, who'd ya think?" Griffin answered. "Cap wants you down in his room, pronto."

"Okay," she said. "Come in."

"How about that?" Griffin said to the others as he turned the knob. "For once she doesn't bite my head off."

"On the floor. *Move!*"

Griffin stood paralyzed for a moment, taking it all in. There was more time in a crisis than people realized. Like when he used to quarterback, fading back with the ball, looking for an opening to run through or a free man to pass to. He'd look at the line and see about eight tons of padded beef charging at him, those black antiglare semicircles under their eyes making them look like zombies. Their hands would be groping toward him like claws. But he didn't panic. He waited, looked around, made his move.

And that's what he did now. He saw that Ravensmith bastard yelling at them, his hand anchored at his chin with an arrow riding the drawn bowstring. He saw the fucking nigger giant with a dumb sword in one hand and a .38 Dan Wesson Model 15-2 VH in the other. He saw the pretty bitch kneeling on the floor next to Angel, a knife pressing into her throat. Three of them against four of us. But the nigger had the gun.

He felt the adrenaline swirling through him. Just like the state championship game against Clayton. All they needed now was fucking cheerleaders. He thought of how angry Rhino would be and what he was like when he was angry. Then a funny image popped into his mind from nowhere. It was a picture of Sylvester Stallone in the ring facing another nigger. Sly was giving him the cold stare and saying, "Go for it!"

So that's what Griffin did.

He nudged the safety on the crossbow as he zagged off to the side, hearing Kelly and Danton following his lead. He pivoted toward Blackjack, wanting to take out the gun first. But even as his finger tensed around the trigger, he heard the loud popping sound and the tugging at his chest as the bullet burrowed through his heart. The last thing he saw was his arrow whacking into the ceiling. Then he felt his sphincter muscles weaken and his bladder open, his pants filling with warm liquids. He knew he was dying and wanted to say something memorable as his last words, but all he could manage was, "Shit." It didn't matter. No one heard him anyway.

Danton was giggling as he hefted his spear, not sure who to throw it at. Before he decided, Eric planted an arrow in his chest. Danton

213

dropped heavily to the floor, his eyes open and still startled at the suddenness of death.

Just as Eric released his arrow, Kelly Furst snatched the Remington .41-caliber rim-fire derringer from her pocket and squeezed off a round at Eric. The bullet chopped through the bow before whizzing past Eric's ear. Before she could fire the second round, Blackjack's gun jumped in his hand again and Kelly was flipped off her feet and into the wall, her head thudding with a dull echo.

Angel didn't struggle, didn't make a move. Tracy kept the blade's edge snug against the windpipe, discouraging any involvement.

"Let's go," Blackjack said urgently. "Security will be here in a couple minutes to investigate the gunshot. You remember what BeBop said?"

Eric ignored him, walking quickly to Griffin's prone body, prying the stiff fingers from his crossbow. He grabbed the arrows too. "Okay. Now we can go."

"'Hold the pickles, hold the lettuce, special orders don't upset us . . .'" Tracy was lying on the 400-year-old bed, her hands clasped behind her head, trying to remember jingles from television commercials. If she closed her eyes, she could clearly see the happy teenage faces marching behind the counter of a Burger King.

She opened her eyes, awkwardly adjusting herself to sit up more, afraid she might drift off to sleep. This would be the worst possible time for sleep.

"'Bud-weiser,'" she sang softly. "'This Bud's for you.'" She looked at her watch again. It was still a 5:23 A.M. Through the window she could see the morning light starting to freckle the Halo. Abruptly she stopped singing about Budweiser and sang, "Somewherrre, over the Halo." The cane Eric had made for her was stretched out on the bed next to her. She pulled it closer. "Come here, Toto."

She studied her watch again. 5:24. What could be keeping them? The longer they waited, the more danger they were in. Surely, they knew that.

After they'd snatched Angel from her room, Blackjack had convinced Eric to let him take her back to the ship. "I can make her talk there, man," he'd said, his smooth black face shining with sweat. "And talk she will."

Eric had hesitated, but finally agreed. "It would be safer."

The calmness with which they'd discussed what was obviously the torture of Angel chilled Tracy. Despite the gruesome stories Eric had told her about Angel, Tracy had trouble seeing herself as part of a gang of torturers. Especially of a woman. Her feminist instincts reacted against it. Wasn't she just helping men abuse a woman. Okay, silly in a way, but in another way, maybe not so silly.

Even sillier, Tracy found herself a little in awe of Angel. The small slender Vietnamese woman seemed so damn confident, so in

215

control. Even if she was doing evil and cruel things, she was doing what she wanted the way she wanted. For the first time she understood a little of how Blackjack must have felt when he'd decided to become a pirate. Like he was shrugging out of a heavy harness of what others expected of you, of what you expected of yourself. Now you could do anything!

What impressed Tracy most about Angel was that she was not afraid of anything. She crossed all moral boundaries without hesitation. Stealing, mutilation, murder—nothing was too far. Not that Tracy would want to venture in that nether land herself, still it made her jealous that others could so easily.

Even physically, Angel was superior. Goddamned flips and somersaults and handsprings like some circus acrobat. Eric had warned her that Angel was an accomplished gymnast, but Tracy had thought that meant a few pirouettes on the beam or that she could stand on her head for five minutes. She'd had no idea.

Tracy stroked the wood of the cane. Once part of an airplane, it had flown through clouds. This wood had learned the ways of lightness; so had Angel. But Tracy was even more earthbound than ever. Not only would she never do handsprings like Angel—who was at least four years older, damn it—but she wouldn't even be able to walk lightly anymore. She'd drag her shattered hip around after the rest of her body like a shy and distant relative.

"'Mmmm mmmm, good,'" Tracy sang,

"'mmmm mmmm, good. That's what Campbell's soup is. Mmmm mmmm, good.'" Where the devil was Eric? When Blackjack had hustled Angel off to *The Argo,* Eric had decided to scout around Liar's Cove a bit, see if anybody knew anything about Dirk Fallows.

So the two men had gone off and left the gimpy woman to tend the home fires while one tortured another woman and the other looked for his kidnapped son.

And she sang commercials and wondered if she'd ever see television again. Christ.

A knock on the door made her snap up Eric's loaded crossbow that he'd left with her.

"Coming through," Eric's voice filtered through the door as he entered. He finished chewing something, swallowed, and said, "Hi."

"What're you eating?"

He smiled. "Peanut butter on a Ritz cracker. Some guy is selling them down in the courtyard. Had people lined up around the building like they were buying tickets to the mainland." He offered her one. "Cost me the whole roll of duct tape for three of them."

Tracy took the offered cracker with its thin smear of peanut butter. She could see the chips of peanuts. "Crunchy," she said appreciatively as she waved it under her nose and inhaled deeply. The smell opened the salivary glands at the back of her tongue. She bit a small corner off. Not too much at once. Make it last. The Ritz cracker was a little stale, but it didn't matter. She

217

chewed slowly, nodding her head. "Oh God, it's almost better than sex."

"And more fattening."

Tracy eyed Eric as she finished off the remains of the cracker. "Any luck?"

"Not yet. Somebody thinks they know somebody who has a friend who may know something if I've got something worth trading for the information. They're just jerking my chain." He settled into a plush chair, a 1920s reproduction of a seventeenth-century French chair to match the beds. He looked pensive as he ran his finger along his scar and stared out the window at the orange tentacles of dawn creeping along the Halo.

Tracy thought he looked disappointed, hurt, and for a moment she wondered if she'd done something wrong. Or was he just reacting to lack of news about Fallows and Timmy? Her own heart clenched at the sight of his anguish, and she felt good realizing that her involvement with Eric was an acrobatic feat that Angel would never be able to duplicate—one that required more emotional agility and had more danger than any amount of leaping and tumbling.

Almost as if he knew what she was thinking, Eric stood up, walked over to her, and kissed her on the cheek. Then on the lips. Suddenly Tracy remembered that she, too, knew the ways of lightness, of flying. She kissed him back.

He sat next to her on the edge of the bed. They were both quiet for a few minutes. Tracy

218

hummed the theme to the McDonald's commercial.

"What do you think he's doing to her?" she finally asked.

Eric polished the brass mechanism of his crossbow with the corner of the blanket. "Remind me to find a hunk of wax for the bowstring before we leave this place."

"You're not answering the question. What do you think he's doing to her?"

"Whatever it takes."

"Torture, right?"

He shrugged. "She won't offer the information for free."

"Jesus, Eric, what have we become?"

Eric looked over his shoulder at Tracy, her young face wrinkled with concern and guilt. She was pulling at a piece of skin around her cuticle, studying it as if she were performing brain surgery. Eric spoke in a low, steady voice, lifting her chin up so their eyes were locked. "I told you about Angel. But I spared you some of the details because I thought it better if you didn't know. Maybe I was wrong." He took a deep breath. "You have to remember that she was a self-made woman of great wealth in Vietnam. Nothing stood in her way. I've seen some of the people who tried to resist her, people Angel 'persuaded' to give her information. She personally cut the eyelids off a sixty-eight-year-old woman who wouldn't tell where her son, a business rival of Angel, was hiding. She sewed together the lips of one of her servants

219

because he told his cousin how much she'd spent on a pair of shoes. She didn't like her employees to give anything away about her."

Tracy swallowed. "I'm not sure that justifies us."

"Maybe not. But don't worry, she's tough but not stupid. She knows she has no choice but to tell Blackjack everything."

"I just can't believe Blackjack would do that kind of thing. He's a doctor, for Christ's sake, even if he is playing at being a pirate."

Eric smiled, smoothed a strand of hair from her forehead. "You underestimate him, Trace, like you sometimes underestimate yourself. People can be hard when they have to. Like that home run swing you cracked against Angel's spine when she dashed for the door. Ever thought you could do that?"

"I wasn't thinking at the time."

"Exactly. Your instincts took over when your conscience didn't want to deal with the problem. You're going to find that happening more and more from now on."

She frowned distastefully. "That's a horrible thought, Eric."

"Perhaps."

Another knocking at the door. "It's me," Blackjack said. His voice seemed different. The impish lilt in it was gone. It sounded flat and drained. "Coming through."

The door opened and he shoved Angél into the room, pulling the door closed behind him.

"Christ," Tracy gasped, wincing at the sight of Angel.

Angel stood in the middle of the room, her eyes glaring defiantly. She resembled a small animal that had been chased through thorny thickets until she could run no longer. Her mouth was bracketed by crooked lines of dried blood down her chin that made her look a little like a ventriloquist's dummy. A large blue bruise swelled under her right eye, stretching the skin taut. Her narrow neck was bruised in a pattern of four fingers on one side of the throat and a thumb imprint on the other side.

"Keep him away from me," she screamed, pointing at Blackjack. Her accent was more pronounced than before. "He is crazy. He tried to kill me." She rubbed the bruises on her throat.

Blackjack looked away from her. Guiltily, Tracy thought. Flopping down into a chair, he plucked a pen and pad from his pocket and tossed them onto the bed between Eric and Tracy. "She's ready."

"Yes, I will draw your map," Angel sneered. "But I will also draw one for Rhino. He will kill all of you."

Eric handed her the small pad and Bic pen. "Right now, Rhino's the last person you'll want to see. If he finds out you killed Alabaster and stole the map behind his back, he'll do things to you beyond even *your* imagination."

She stared at him silently, then opened the

221

note pad and began drawing.

"I wanted her to do the map in front of all of us," Blackjack said. "That way we can keep everything aboveboard. Okay?"

Eric gave him a funny smile. "Appreciate the thought."

"Let's just get it over with and get the hell out of here," Tracy said.

Angel scribbled away on the pad.

"One other question," Tracy said, standing. "What do we do with her once we have the map?"

"I promised her we'd release her," Blackjack said. "Any problems with that?"

Angel stopped writing, looked up at Eric.

Eric turned toward Tracy. "You have any problem with that?"

"I don't know," Tracy answered, avoiding looking in Angel's direction. She could feel the woman's dynamic presence there like a hot wind. "How do we know the map will be accurate? She may be lying."

"Good point," Eric said.

"I destroyed the original map," Angel said. "But this is the same. I swear."

"You'll pardon me," Tracy said, "but your assurances aren't quite enough. I mean, what happens when we go to God knows where and find nothing there but a couple of iguanas sunning themselves on the hood of an Edsel?"

Blackjack nodded. "There's an element of chance involved, sure. But she also knows that we'll make sure Rhino knows what she'd done with Alabaster. That'll mean he'll be after her as well as us. California just ain't that big anymore. Where's she going to hide?"

"We can always take her with us?" Eric suggested. He was looking at Tracy in such a way that she felt as if the decision was up to her. She would decide Angel's fate.

"You promised to let me go if I drew map," Angel hollered. "You made bargain."

"Did you?" Tracy asked Blackjack.

Blackjack shrugged.

"Okay, we'll stick to the deal." Tracy shifted her eyes to meet Angel's. "And we'll rely on her good sense, knowing what will happen to her if she lies."

Angel bent back over the map, the Bic fine-point pen scratching against the paper.

Outside the door and window, the constant sound of the unending party continued. Merchants still hawked their wares, visitors guzzled BeBop's Brew.

When she was done, Angel stood up and threw the pad into Blackjack's face. "You black bastard."

The wire binding left a slight welt on his cheek, but he ignored that as he studied the map, grinning. "Just a couple days inland from here. No sweat." He held the pad out to Eric. "Wanna see?"

Eric shook his head. "Let's get started. You go back to the ship and gather the crew. Tracy and I

223

will go into the marketplace and pick up a few things for the trip."

"Right."

"What about me?" Angel said.

Eric pointed at the door. "I'd head south. Rhino's bound to figure it all out sooner or later."

She started to say something just as the door flew open, banging into the wall. A squad of five armed men crowded around the door, each wearing the Hearst Castle T-shirt that identified them as BeBop's security force. They were pointing an assortment of sharp weapons at Eric and the others in the room.

Behind them, hovering over their shoulders, Rhino rocked anxiously, thrusting an accusing finger at them. "There they are. There!"

Angel's movements were explosive, like those of a bat discovered behind a shutter. She ran toward a second-story window, did a handspring onto the floor that propelled her feet-first through the glass and onto the stone terrace. Without hesitation, she vaulted over the side, leaping into the large tree nearby.

"Get her!" Rhino yelled, his voice trembling with rage.

Two of the security squad finally shook off their amazement long enough to race across the room and lean out over the balcony. A couple arrows were fired into the rustling tree, but they were swallowed harmlessly by thick branches and leaves.

Even inside they could hear the slap of

Angel's bare feet racing away.

"Let her go," a bearded member of the squad said, turning back to Tracy, Blackjack, and Eric. "At least we still have these three."

"Kill them!" Rhino ordered. "Kill them now!"

17

"I warned you," BeBop smiled. "I really did."

They were standing amidst a crowd of people gathered around the elaborate indoor pool northeast of the Casa Grande. The room housing the giant pool filled with reflected orange light from the high arched windows along the wall. The floor and walls were completely covered in blue glass tiles imported from Murano, Italy, causing the room to shimmer eerily, as if they were all underwater rather than standing next to a pool.

Spaced around the pool were eight Carrara marble sculptures commissioned of Carlo Freter of Pietrasanta, Italy, just for this room. Each was a reproduction of a famous classical work.

BeBop was leaning against "Diana and the Deer." Someone with a felt pen had vandalized the statue, drawing nipples where the breasts were covered by the white marble folds of her dress. Black pubic hairs were scribbled between her legs.

"Didn't I warn them, Tsetse?"

The young boy sat against the wall, balancing his blow gun on his knees. "Yeah, BeBop, you warned 'em. I heard you."

BeBop looked at Eric, Tracy, and Blackjack, then sighed like a parent disappointed with his children's behavior. With a grin, he strummed his guitar and began to sing, improvising an off-key tune. "Oh, baby, I warned ya/Tole ya not to be no asshole/ When you visiting Hearst Cas-tle." He laughed. "Not bad, huh? The acoustics in this place are awesome."

"Let's get on with it," Rhino said, standing with what was left of his crew. His eyes were rimmed with red and his lumpish body trembled, even while standing still. Whatever demons had invaded his system after passing through the Halo seemed to have accelerated until Rhino jittered like a man standing on a live wire. It was as if his entire nervous system were disintegrating. Occasionally he snapped his rubber band, but more out of habit than to control himself. He was past that now. The flesh on the inside of his wrist was bruised and raw, but he didn't feel anything there when he snapped the rubber band and shouted, "I want them executed."

This brought excited murmurs from the early morning crowd. An execution would be an entertaining way to start the day.

Eric took a step toward BeBop, saw Tsetse shift his blow gun at the movement. Eric wasn't

228

about to try anything, not with BeBop's security force fanned out around him. One of the T-shirted guards was holding Eric's crossbow, Blackjack's saber and gun, and Tracy's bow.

"Rhino's right," Eric said. "Let's get on with it. Starting with why we were brought here?"

"You know why you were fucking brought here!" Rhino shrieked, making a fist of his delicate fingers. "You kidnapped Angel and murdered three members of my crew."

"How do you plead, gang?" BeBop asked them with a dramatic strum of his guitar.

Eric shook his head. "I don't know what he's talking about."

"You know goddamn well what I'm talking about!" Rhino blasted.

"Except for a brief excursion to our boat and one for some peanut butter on Ritz crackers, we were in our room the whole night."

"Yeah, I know the place," BeBop nodded. "Gino used to own a pizza parlor in Fresno. Now it's peanut butter on Ritz."

Rhino reached for the .38 tucked in his waistband.

"Whoa," BeBop said, holding up his hands. One of the guards with a shotgun stepped forward and nudged Rhino's arm. Rhino shoved the gun back into his waistband. "No violence, Rhino. Not yet."

"I think I can clear this matter up," Eric said. "Are there any witnesses to the crimes?"

Laughter from the crowd rattled the windows.

BeBop explained. "Those who might have seen something, probably can't remember what they saw last night. And those who can remember don't want to get involved and get their throats slit some night."

"But your own men saw Angel in their room," Rhino sputtered. "She'd been *beaten.*"

BeBop turned to the head of his security force. "Tony?"

"Yeah," Tony said. "She was in their room. I only saw a glimpse of her, but she was banged up a bit."

"I told you," Rhino said. "Now let me have them."

"Mind if I ask a question?" Eric said.

BeBop shrugged. "Your witness, Mr. Mason."

"Tony, was Angel bound in any way. Hand cuffed or tied up?"

"Nope."

Eric turned back to BeBop. "The explanation is simple. Angel had a map to a cache of weapons left over from when the government was confiscating them after the first quake. She was trying to make a deal with us behind Rhino's back. He found out, sent his crew up to get her. Angel panicked, killed them, sustaining bruises in the struggle. Then she came to our room to try to sell us the map. That's why she ran when she saw Rhino."

BeBop's eyes lit up at mention of the weapons cache, knowing what power the owner of that map would have. He picked out a few notes from "Stairway To Heaven," trying to look casual. "And where is this map now?"

"She took it with her out the window," Blackjack answered.

"Pity."

"It's all *bullshit!*" Rhino wailed. "She didn't have any map. They kidnapped her and killed my crew."

"If she didn't have any map," Eric said, "why would we want to kidnap her."

"Because you wanted—"

"Enough!" BeBop yelled, banging on the strings of his guitar. "I don't give a rat's ass who's right anymore. This ain't the fucking Supreme Court, Rhino, so don't come bitching to me. All I care about is that this place remains peaceful so business can be conducted so I can get my cut. I got overhead, man." He hooked a thumb at his security squad. "You think these guys follow my orders because they like my music? Hell, no. They get their cut of my cut. See?" He took a deep breath, stared into what was once a luxurious swimming pool. Now the water that filled the pool was rancid with vegetation. So much junk had been thrown into the pool that one could hardly see the water through the broken bicycles, empty cans, newspapers, cartons, and other debris that had been tossed in as if it were a giant garbage can. BeBop pointed at the pool. "That's where you're gonna settle this. In there."

"What?" Rhino asked.

"You two." He pointed at Rhino, then at

231

Eric. "You two had the most to say, now you're gonna get a chance to settle up. Let's go. In the pool. The one who comes out alive wins the argument. Those with the loser, get to take his body and get the fuck out of Liar's Cove."

"That's ridiculous," Rhino protested.

"It's not up for debate, Rhino. You've been a good customer, but I've got lots of customers, and they know that BeBop takes care of them. So get your dumpy little fanny in that pool."

Eric didn't say anything. He began stripping off his shirt, kicking off his boots. The improvised bandages that Tracy had had wound around his chest had been replaced by Nurse Havczech, but Eric could still feel the ache of his wound underneath.

"For Christ's sake, BeBop," Blackjack protested. "You can see that he's wounded. Let me take his place."

"No way, José. You let him do the talking, now he's gotta do the fighting." He glanced over at Rhino, who had not yet made a move. "Come on, big fella. Everybody's waiting."

Rhino looked confused for a moment, the gnarled half of his face making him resemble the statues scattered around the pool. Finally a small smile cracked the good half of his face, his lips spreading slowly like the splitting seam of a football. He shrugged out of his neat double-breasted jacket, then leaned one hand against "Diana and the Deer" while removing his patent leather loafers. He wore no socks.

Eric walked to the edge of the pool, thinking

232

Rhino was ready. But the bigger man continued to strip. He peeled off his shirt and pants to the unified gasping of the crowd, who were shocked to discover the pattern of scarring on his face continued down his entire body. Half of his body was covered with the thick slabs of scarred flesh like the wrinkled hide of a rhinoceros. The effect was particularly hideous because the normal half of his body sprouted thick matted hair. The scarred half was slick and hairless.

Rhino stood only in his boxer shorts, facing the crowd with that half-smile. He stepped out of his shorts, totally naked.

This brought an even louder murmur of surprise, chorused by his own crew. Rhino's penis, given a fifty-fifty chance of going with either half of his body, had chosen the deformed half. It was a twisted white stub of swirling scar tissue, like a cigar that had been angrily stubbed out. One buttock drooped heavily under the extra weight of the scarred skin.

Without hesitation, Rhino stepped to the edge of the pool and jumped in. His body splashed aside a small circle of the floating garbage. He stood looking up at Eric, the water lapping his chest. An empty can of Coors bumped his back.

"Now *that*," BeBop said with admiration, "is entertainment." He signaled to Tsetse, who scampered to his feet and brought over the Donnie and Marie Osmond lunch bucket. BeBop took a tiny snort, closed the pail, and waved at Eric.

"Let's go, bashful."

Eric leaped into the pool five feet away from Rhino. Being shorter than Rhino, the water splashed against his chin as he stood and waited. The stench of the putrid water was nauseating, but he tried to ignore it. Instead he concentrated on the scarred lump of a man wading toward him.

"Okay," BeBop said. "Let the duel begin. Last one out is a dead egg."

The crowd began to cheer.

Rhino was steaming toward him like a full-speed tanker. His huge bulk swept the water aside in great waves. The blanket of trash that coated the pool rolled in rhythm with the swells. Rhino's slender fingers were held out in front of him like mechanical claws.

Eric waited, sliding his feet backward along the bottom of the pool. His feet often nudged unseen debris and he was not anxious to step on anything sharp. The thick coating of slime under his feet made it hard for him to keep his balance.

Rhino seemed to have the same trouble, slipping twice as he plowed toward Eric. Once his head went under the water as he flailed for balance. When he came back up he spit the water from his mouth, including a piece of white styrofoam from a coffee cup. A thick string of dark algae hung from one scarred ear.

"Move to the shallow end, Eric," Tracy advised, hollering over the hoots and catcalls of the crowd.

Eric noticed the people clustered around the pool, more coming in all the time. Some were kneeling, shouting encouragement to the gladiator of their choice, keeping their throats moist with mugs of BeBop's Brew. No matter how desperate their own lives became, people needed distractions, needed to see the life and death struggles performed by others. Eric imagined the cavemen, after a hard day's hunting and fighting, returning home only to reenact it all with paintings on the wall. Now that TV, movies, theater, records, and professional sports were gone, what else was left but this kind of hideous combat.

BeBop watched the proceedings with an amused grin. To him it was a business strategy, nothing more. That his clients were entertained by it all was a bonus. Eric thought he even saw a glimmer of regret in BeBop's eyes that he hadn't thought of charging them all to watch the fight.

"The shallow end!" Tracy repeated.

Eric didn't have time to tell her he had more of an advantage in deeper water than a taller man. In shallow water, the bigger man could use his weight and height with more leverage. In the deeper water, that advantage was taken away. Eric waited until Rhino was almost on top of him before diving under the water and swimming toward the deep end. He didn't dare open his eyes in this poisoned mess, relying instead on his sense of direction. When his head popped out of the water again, his feet dangled under him in deep water.

The crowd was booing, yelling "coward" and "chickenshit" at him.

Rhino was swimming toward him now, his huge legs kicking a geyser of water behind him with each stroke.

This time Eric was ready. He waited until Rhino was within three feet, the big man's small hands reaching out of the water for Eric's throat. Suddenly Eric ducked under the water, curling into a ball, then kicking out both feet at once. They struck Rhino's stomach, sinking a few inches into the blubbery flesh.

Rhino doubled over, his face slapping the water, air bubbling out of his mouth in a muffled grunt.

Eric coiled his legs again, sprang them out at Rhino. They caught him in the chest this time, propelling Rhino backward a little. Eric could hear the man's garbled groan even underwater. He started to coil his legs again for another kick.

But he was too slow.

Rhino snagged one of Eric's ankles and yanked him through the water like a hooked tuna. Eric was two feet under the surface on his back as he was dragged forward, water forcing itself up his nose. He tried to twist around, kicking at Rhino's hands with his free foot. But it was no use. Rhino's grip was too strong.

The power pulling him along was so fierce that some of the floating garbage from the surface was sucked down into the whirlpool, swirling around Eric's face. This is what it must feel like to be flushed down a toilet, he thought.

Then he was no longer being pulled, and the hands around his ankle were now fastened like fat leeches around his neck, crushing his windpipe while holding him under the water. He had lost all his air seconds ago and was now functioning on pure adrenaline, fighting the sharp pain in his empty lungs. The arrow hole in his chest opened up and he could feel his blood oozing into the warm swampy pool. Absurdly he worried about his wound getting infected even as he tried to fight his way to the surface.

He pried at the fingers around his throat, but they didn't budge. It was as if they were nailed to his neck. His eyes were open now and he could see Rhino's gruesome face hovering just above the surface, hear Tracy and Blackjack screaming behind him, begging Eric to do *something*.

And Eric did.

His cupped hands shot up out of the water and clapped together on both of Rhino's ears, bursting the eardrums. Rhino's roar of pain vibrated through the water. But still Rhino squeezed tighter. Eric felt his chest heaving involuntarily, felt the rush of warm water through his nostrils, flushing down his throat. He had to try again.

This time he launched his thumbs straight up into Rhino's eyes, digging the thumbnails deep into the eyeballs. Rhino's good eye flattened under the pressure, but that black marble of an eye on the damaged side of his face didn't move. It was as hard as a pearl, petrified. Eric

237

dug harder.

Rhino's grip eased a little, then a little more. Eric was floating to the top. He broke the surface, sucked his lungs full of air, and heaved his weight into his thumbs.

But Rhino clamped his hands around Eric's wrists and easily pried them away. The enormous strength of the man surprised Eric. He tried to yank his hands free, but Rhino pulled them apart as easily as snapping a wishbone.

With a loud growl, Rhino suddenly reached down, grabbed a handful of Eric's chest bandage and a handful of pants and plucked Eric out of the water, raising him over his head. He threw him straight at the blue tiled corner of the pool like a child trying to crack open a clam by hurling it at a sharp rock.

Eric twisted slightly in midair, allowing his muscular back to smash against the hard edge of the pool, absorbing most of the shock. His head grazed the corner, sending five hundred volts of pain into his skull, but there was no serious damage. Dazed, Eric slid from the edge under the water to the bottom of the pool. His left foot landed on a piece of glass that sliced through the callouses on the ball of his foot. The pain jangled his nerves and sent an icy eel slithering through his stomach.

He forced his eyes open, peered through the murky slush. Ten feet away he saw Rhino's tree stump legs churning toward him. Eric dropped his hands to the bottom of the pool, felt gingerly for the glass that had cut his foot. Maybe a weapon, he hoped. His fingers bumped a high-top Nike sneaker, Volume I of *Webster's Third International Dictionary* A–G, a broken amber globe that used to belong to the lights around the pool. Too unwieldy, he thought, brushing it aside. Then his hands touched something else. At first he thought it was some kind of electrical wire, but it was too rigid. Then he recognized it: a wire coat hanger.

The legs were almost on him now. He didn't want to be caught short of breath again, so he fished up the coat hanger and kicked off the side of the pool, swimming furiously to the deepest part. When his head bobbed up again, he saw Rhino doing an easy breaststroke toward him. Eric hooked the hanger in his waistband to keep it out of sight.

"Hey, Ravensmith," BeBop warned. "You can't keep running, man. We can't spend the rest of the day here settling this one dispute. I got a whole fucking castle to run here. You either fight or"—he nodded toward Tsetse—"my buddy here is gonna stick your face full of pins."

Tsetse pulled a pin from his fishing hat and thumbed it into the end of his blowgun.

BeBop grabbed Tsetse's wrist and turned it so he could read the boy's watch. "I'll give you both another five minutes. After that I'll have to award the match to my old buddy Rhino, based on aggressiveness. And you and your friends will be history. Understood?"

"Understood," Eric responded, but didn't move.

Rhino grinned as he paddled closer, speaking out of one side of his mouth. "Don't worry, Ravensmith. You don't even have five minutes."

Eric treaded water for the twenty seconds it took for Rhino to get within five feet of him. Then he dove under the water, stretching the hanger at the hook and the middle of the bottom bar into an elongated diamond, making an opening he hoped would be large enough. His eyes were stinging from the dirty water as he swam, barely able to make out his target through the haze.

Rhino swiveled his head around, whipping it from side to side as he searched for Eric while treading water. He couldn't see anything through the floating garbage. Viciously he brushed away a soggy *TV Guide* that was piggyback on a tree branch. He looked over his shoulder at BeBop. "He's running again, damn it. I want—"

But before he could tell the young musician and lord of Liar's Cove what he wanted, Eric exploded out of the water and jammed the hanger over his head, pulling it tight around the ragged throat, and twisting off the slack wire. Rhino's head jerked back as he clawed behind him for a piece of Eric. Eric leaned back, his knees lodged hard against Rhino's spine as he pulled on the hanger, constantly twisting the wire tighter. With each twist the black wire bit deeper into Rhino's windpipe.

Rhino's sputtering was a choked hiss. His small hands flailed blindly behind him, occasionally brushing some part of Eric's body, but not enough for those iron fingers to grab hold. He tried shaking his attacker off, but Eric rode him like a bucking bronco, yanking hard on the hanger, twisting the wire tighter and tighter.

The normal half of Rhino's face turned red, then white, then blue, but the scarred half maintained its lifeless marble color. With the terror of death slowly enveloping him, Rhino gave one last mournful cry, shrugging his shoulders like Atlas hefting off the world. Eric flipped up into the air, still holding onto the hook of the hanger with one hand. As he came back down again, Rhino was struggling to loosen the hanger with one hand, and reaching for Eric with the other. He managed to snag a handful of Eric's hair and was pulling him over his shoulder.

Eric had lost position, his knees no longer wedged into Rhino's huge back. He felt the stronger man's insistent power pulling him forward by the hair. He tried tightening the hanger more, but he was losing leverage there too. If Rhino managed to get both hands on him again, Eric knew he was done. He didn't have the strength—or time—to fight off another attack from those deadly hands.

Desperately, Eric held onto the hanger with one hand and dug his other hand into Rhino's face, trying to gouge at the eyes as he had before. Only his hands kept slipping from the rubbery scar tissue. Finally he clamped on to the thick ridge of flesh hanging over Rhino's black marble eye and pulled. A hunk of skin came off in his hands!

He could hear the horrified screams of some of the crowd, Tracy among them, and the howls of laughter from the others, drowning Rhino's own tortured wail. The shock of pain and the gushing of blood into his eye, distracted Rhino long enough for Eric to climb back into position. With five quick turns he twisted the hanger tight enough to cut off all the air.

Rhino began to sink into the deep water, weakly clutching at the wire and Eric. Eric stayed in place, knees pressed into the back, leaning backward, pulling on the wire. The muscles and veins bulged on Eric's arms and neck like bridge cables. He gulped a mouthful of air as they went under, Rhino fighting now in slow motion, a dying lump of animal raging against death.

Then nothing.

Eric didn't dismount immediately. He waited, holding his breath, ignoring the stinging in his eyes as he watched through the filthy waters Rhino's lifeless arms float out to the side. When he was satisfied that Rhino wasn't faking, Eric kicked off the dead man's back and broke surface, swimming lazily to the edge of the pool. Tracy and Blackjack helped him out of the water.

The crowd was alternately cheering and booing. Eric saw goods exchanging hands—cartridges, arrows, walnuts, salt—as losers paid their bets.

Eric looked at BeBop. "You owe me a bath."

BeBop's face clenched suddenly with anger. "I don't owe you jackshit, pal. You're alive. Consider yourself lucky."

Eric leveled his stare at the young man, his lips curled into a grim imitation of a smile.

BeBop flinched a little, then shrugged. "All right. You earned it, man. Least I can do for a really big show." He turned around and faced Rhino's crew. "You can fish the whale meat out of the pool and get out of here. You've got an hour." He waved the head of his security force to his side, speaking loud enough for the crowd to appreciate his words. "I want these three to have the run of Liar's Cove for the rest of the day. Anything they want. Within reason." He laughed, wagging a finger at Eric. The crowd cheered again. "Now let's get the hell out of this cesspool," he said, and spit into the pool.

The crowd began pressing and shoving through the doors. As they did, BeBop, a diplomatic smile pasted on his face, stepped up to Eric and whispered, "You'd be wise to be gone from here by morning. And I don't want to see any of you back here for a long, long time. You're bad for business."

18.

Angel liked the dark. It was the only time she felt safe. In control. While others feared the dark, violated its purity with cowardly light, she thought of it as a kind of thick liquid through which she alone could move. Her own special magic.

She hunkered now in the room shared by Eric, Tracy, and Blackjack, her left hand clutching a stack of six throwing stars, a balisong knife in her pocket. They had been easy to steal from the old man who sold such specialty items in the courtyard. It was fortunate she had not been caught, for BeBop demanded immediate execution of anyone caught stealing within Liar's Cove. Though they were mostly thieves and murderers anyway, he was proud to provide a place where criminals could relax their guard momentarily. But she had not been worried about capture. After all, she had been stealing since she was three years old. Not out of

245

necessity, of course, like the ragtag children of her country. No, she did it merely out of desire. The challenge. Her parents had provided her with plenty of everything. The best that Saigon society could offer. But young Suzette, who would amaze her friends with magnificent gymnastic feats, did not want what was offered. She wanted only what she could take. And she took plenty.

Now she would take three lives.

She had already drawn the heavy curtains to keep out the light, and moved the lamp to another table to confuse them when they entered. Eric would immediately suspect a trap, so she would have to kill him first. Then the black man who thought he was so clever. Finally Eric's woman. If they were still back in Vietnam, in the years when she had her own empire and many men to do her bidding, she would kill them slowly, with special attention to Eric. But now there was no time. She would kill them quickly, lucky for them.

She could almost laugh at the irony of running from Vietnam—both sides wanted her dead—only to end up in a California as ravaged as Vietnam ever had been. The stupid Americans living here thought they were so clever surviving the natural catastrophes. But this was how it had been to live back home for many years. Vietnamese children of six had more survival skills than most of these bloated Americans.

She crouched behind the bed, waiting. If she

had learned anything in her adventurous life, it was the virtue of waiting for your prey to come to you. She ignored the various pains that rattled through her body. The dive out the window and leap to the tree had not been without costs. The skin on her left palm had been raked off when she'd grabbed the branch awkwardly. The bark had sandpapered her skin into a raw mush. Her shoulder ached where the muscle had ripped when she'd dropped twenty feet out of the tree. Her lower back muscles burned with a long thick bruise where Tracy had smacked her with her cane, almost knocking her unconscious. She would take special interest in repaying the bitch for that. Perhaps death would be too kind. Yes, maybe mutilation would be more appropriate. Once she had cut off the toe of a man who refused to give her information she wanted to sell. He still refused, playing the brave patriotic soldier. She then forced him to eat his own toe. He told her everything.

She smiled, passing time by deciding which parts of Tracy to amputate.

They were less than thirty feet from the door to their room when Blackjack stopped.

"If we're taking off in the morning to follow the map, I'd better get back to the ship and get my crew ready. We'll need them to help carry the guns back."

"Good idea," Eric said, dripping water onto

the floor. "Still have the map?"

Blackjack patted his back pocket and pulled out the little memo pad. He flipped it through the air to Eric. "Here, you hold on to it."

"Shouldn't I trust you?"

"This has nothing to do with trust. Anybody finds out about it, I don't want them coming after me. I figure after the way you handled Rhino, you can handle just about anybody."

Crowds of people were still winding through the corridors, some just waking up, some just heading for bed. It reminded Eric of an old zombie movie or of red-eyed gamblers in Las Vegas.

Eric pinched the notebook between finger and thumb to avoid getting it wet and handed it to Tracy. She tucked it away in one of the extra pockets on the thigh of her pants. Rachel Loeb had given them to her after Blackjack had cut up her jeans to treat her hip wound. They were some designer's fashionable imitation of a carpenter's pants, but without the bib. They even had a loop for a hammer. It had pleased Tracy at the time to discover the pants were a size too large for her, until Rachel informed Tracy that they were also too large for her. But she'd immediately liked Rachel when she'd laughed and said, "It took an earthquake to keep me on my diet."

"Hey, Tracy," Blackjack said, "you still with us?"

"Huh? Oh, right. I'm just tired, letting my mind wander. Now that Rhino's dead and

Angel's gone, there's nothing more to worry about." She laughed. "I guess I'm just not used to relaxing anymore."

Eric squeezed her shoulder affectionately. "Take a nap, you'll feel better."

"Great, a nap. Then I can have my milk and cookies. Honestly, guys, every time I make a comment or an observation, it doesn't mean I need help deciding what to do next. Christ."

Blackjack held up his hands and grinned. "Uh-oh, domestic squabble at twelve o'clock high and coming fast. This is where my people have an old saying: Feet don't fail me now." He spun around and headed toward the exit, one hand on his saber as it jangled at his side. He waved. "See you back here in a couple hours."

"Right," Eric waved back.

They started back toward the room.

When they were ten feet from the door, Eric stopped. "Listen, Trace, I think I'm going to go get that bath now, maybe some new clothes for the hike."

She arched one eyebrow. "And where are you going for this bath?"

"The only place you can get them here, Casa del Sol."

"Yeah, that's not all you can get there. Don't bring back anything contagious."

Eric looked her in the eye, knew she was teasing him. "I'll be back in a while. Maybe we can take that nap together."

She smiled, wiped away some of the unidentifiable filth from the pool that was still clinging

249

to his cheek, and kissed him there. "If you still have the energy."

Eric winked, turned, and angled through the crowd toward the exit.

Tracy sighed as she limped toward the door to their room, her cane thumping next to her with each step like a pronouncement: Hear ye, hear ye. This person is permanently crippled.

Watching Eric fight Rhino had exhausted her more than it had Eric. She had strangled her own hands during the battle, grinding the knuckles of her fingers together as if they were Rhino's throat.

She turned the doorknob and entered the dark room. She didn't remember the room being this dark before. Perhaps one of the security force had drawn the curtains when they left last time and she'd been too scared to notice. It didn't matter. She would just open them again.

Or maybe she should leave them closed, tumble into the bed, and sleep. God, that sounded more erotic than sex right now. Sleep.

Suddenly she heard a faint whispering sound, like a long hiss of something flying toward her. An insect, she thought. Then came an explosion of hot pain as something sharp dug into her chest.

Tracy staggered backward, arms windmilling to keep balance. Her cane clattered to the floor and rolled away. It was too dark to see what had struck her, but she grabbed for it with her hands.

Then another hissing sound and something stabbing her right thigh. She dropped to her knees, hands groping along the dark floor for her cane. Finding nothing but blackness.

"I had hoped for all three of you," Angel said. "But this will do. This will do nicely."

Angel's cold voice clawing through the dark was even more terrifying than the pain. She had seen Angel's supple agility at work before, witnessed the woman's power. How could she possibly survive against a woman like this? Tracy felt panicky, as if she were being buried under a truckload of gravel.

With some difficulty, Tracy plucked the throwing star from her chest, jiggling and twisting until it jerked free. It had lodged just above the breast and to the side. The muscle ached, but there was no injury to any internal organs. The one in her thigh was a little more stubborn, but she finally coaxed it out, feeling the warm blood soaking into Rachel Loeb's pants. She gripped one of the stars in her hand as if it were a rock she intended to skip across a pond. She wasn't exactly sure how they were supposed to be thrown, but she didn't care. At least now she had a weapon too.

Tracy shivered, feeling terribly exposed. Despite the darkness, she was sure that Angel could somehow see her plainly, was just toying with her. But if she couldn't, Tracy didn't want to crawl or limp around and tip off her location. She waited, hoping her eyes would eventually adjust to the dark.

But there was no time.

There was hardly any sound at all. A hop, maybe a leap. Then Angel was on top of Tracy. A knee to the chin flipped Tracy onto her back, the throwing stars tumbling out of her hand, scurrying across the floor, and disappearing into the darkness.

Dazed but still conscious, Tracy's hands reached out at the dark figure hovering above her. Everything was in different shades of black now, with Angel being the darkest shadow in the room. Tracy's hands were still groping for some part of Angel that she might wrestle to the ground, when she grabbed the muscular legs straddling her. Suddenly she felt the sting of sharp cold metal slashing the top of her hand open. A second slash caught between the webbing of two fingers and cut deep, bumping bone. She cried out with pain.

Angel dropped onto Tracy like a rock from a cliff. The air whooshed out of Tracy as she felt the smaller woman's knees slam into her chest.

I'm going to die, she realized. Just when she'd thought there was some little safety. Eric had killed Rhino, now it was her turn to die. It was the way of the world. Everything died unexpectedly.

She wondered if that thought had gone through Eric's mind while he was battling Rhino. Had he ever doubted that he would win? He had once told her that he'd been paralyzed with fear the night Fallows had sent someone into his room to assassinate his family. He had stood in his bedroom next to his sleeping wife, knowing someone was coming up the stairs, and had been frozen there, unable to move. The fear had been so great, he'd said, that he'd wanted to die more than experience such fear again. Yet somehow, he had roused himself, had fought the intruder. She hadn't totally believed him, had been unable to accept that Eric Ravensmith had ever felt such fear. He had only been trying to make her feel better. But now she knew he had, and that he had probably felt it again while Rhino held him under the rancid water of that slimy pool. The difference was that he had kept fighting despite the fear. He'd overcome it, battling it with the same ferocity he had Rhino.

And so would she.

Tracy bucked her hips into the air, trying to throw Angel off, but it did no good. All she received for her efforts was a shallow slash across the forehead.

"Careful, my little pretty," Angel cooed, "or I might miss and hit an eye."

Tracy remained still. Except for her left hand, which crabbed along the floor, sliding down her pants to the pocket on her thigh. In the right pocket was the map Angel had drawn. In the left was the small curved knife Eric had made from the steel arches of his boots.

"I have the map here," Tracy said, trying to sound as if she were begging. She didn't have to act too hard. Her hand dipped into the pocket. Slow and easy.

"My, what would dear Eric say if he knew you were bargaining away his precious map? Why, he might shoot you, as he did me."

"Please," Tracy said. The sob in her voice was real.

Angel laughed, flicked her wrist. Tracy felt the blade slice down the side of her neck. It happened so quickly, with such precision, she was reminded of the Japanese cooks at Benihana's. Crazy thought, she realized as her hand eased the blade free.

"Do not despair," Angel said. "Think of this as a test of Eric's devotion. Will he still love you after I've made a few alterations? You should be grateful to me. Not many couples have the chance to discover the extent of their mate's love." The blade whisked through the dark again and Tracy felt the skin on her chin part. "Are your ears pierced?" Angel asked, laughing. "Well, it won't really matter anymore—*uhhnn!*"

The laughing chatter was interrupted by a shocked grunt of pain and realization as Tracy plunged the handmade knife into Angel's stomach, just below the sternum, and sawed through the blouse and skin with all her strength. She braced her wrist with her free hand, forcing the hooked blade down toward the navel. She heard Angel's knife thud to the floor, felt the splash of warm liquid on her own chest. Tracy fought the cloying nausea as she smelled Angel's internal organs sloshing out of her body, spilling onto her blouse. Angel swayed a moment, tried to speak, but managed only a choked rasp. Then she toppled sideways onto the floor.

Tracy dragged herself out from under the corpse, brushing the slippery residue of Angel's innards from her own body as if she thought it too might be alive. She wanted to scream now. Scream so loudly that the whole room would collapse. Scream until the Long Beach Halo shattered like the inner dome of heaven.

Instead, she waited.

19.

Eric tipped the canteen, took a swig of water. "Well, at least we know the map is authentic."

Tracy leaned on her cane. "How do we know that?"

"Angel wouldn't have tried to kill us otherwise."

"*Us?*" Tracy said.

"You were supposed to be the first. She just didn't know how tough you were."

"Neither did I." Tracy lightly touched the cuts on her forehead and chin.

"I did," Eric said, with a trace of pride.

Blackjack looked up into the bright afternoon sun and wiped the sweat from his forehead. "The three of us are so bandaged up we look like those three Revolutionary soldiers in that painting. You know, one carries the flag, one bangs the drum, and one plays the flute or fife or some damn thing."

"That painting is 'The Spirit of '76' by Archibald M. Willard," Eric said.

Blackjack gave him a disgusted look and turned to Tracy. "How do you stand it."

"Lots of patience," she sighed.

The rest of the eight-member crew took the opportunity to sip water and complain about the hilly terrain.

"Time enough for me to take a leak?" Brad Collins asked. He was a young Australian who'd been visiting California for a surfing competition when the quakes hit.

"Sure," Blackjack waved, "take your time and do it right."

Eric pointed back across three hills they had just covered. Atop the farthest one was Hearst Castle. "Quite a sight, huh?"

Tracy shook her head. "It's a shame that all those great art treasures are being destroyed, but I hope we never see the place again."

Blackjack stretched, rolling his neck until the bones cracked into place. "One more hill and you won't be able to see it."

"One more hill and I won't be able to see anything," Tracy laughed.

Eric looked at his watch, then up at the sun. "Probably a good idea if we camp here for the rest of the day."

"What for?" Blackjack asked. "We can cover a lot more ground before the sun goes down."

"That's the point, Blackjack. We don't want to travel during the day. We dehydrate much faster. We don't know how much water there is between here and the weapons, so we have to conserve our supply." He threw his backpack on the ground. "So we sit here in the shade until dark and move out then. Besides, we have a great view of the castle."

"We don't need a great view of the god-damned castle. We need to move our asses over that hill so we can find the weapons. You want to get to Santa Barbara and find your kid, don't you?"

Eric smiled at him. "In time." Eric sat down next to his pack and leaned his crossbow on a nearby rock.

Blackjack was obviously displeased, but shrugged to the rest of the crew who quickly captured some shade for themselves.

They sat silently for more than an hour. Tracy read a book of Persian recipes that Eric had picked up as they left Liar's Cove. It was the only book he could find, but she was pleased. At least it was *something* to read.

Blackjack fretted, anxiously checking the sun, as if he could will it down out of the sky.

Eric closed his eyes and napped, occasionally waking up to check his watch. Finally, he kept his eyes open. He was smiling in a peculiar way.

"You aren't turning funny, are you?" Tracy asked him. "I mean, you don't hear messages from God or anything?"

"What?"

"Well, that shit-eating grin of yours. Did you just make a killing in the stockmarket, or what?"

"No, no. I was just thinking."

"About what?"

"Angel."

"Oh."

"Nothing like that. I was thinking how desperate she was to think she could get away with something so dumb."

"You mean trying to kill me? Hell, she almost made it."

"No, not that. I mean the whole map business."

Blackjack sat up. "What do you mean? You said it was real."

"Did I?" Eric said. He leaned back against his backpack, his hands webbed behind his head. "Did you get a close look at those bruises on her neck, Tracy?"

Tracy was confused. She knew Eric was getting at something, but she didn't know what. Whatever it was, she had a feeling she wasn't going to like the outcome. "Yeah, I saw them."

"C'mon, man," Blackjack said defensively. "I did what I had to do to get the map. You knew what was going on, so don't start accusing me of brutality."

"You miss the point, Blackjack. I'm surprised, too, you being a doctor and all."

"Cut the shit, Eric," Blackjack barked. "What are you getting at?"

"Notice the way the bruises were? With the thumb imprint lower than the top finger?"

Tracy closed her eyes, pictured Angel's neck as if she were about to draw it. "Yeah. That's right. So?"

"So there's only one way she could have gotten bruises like that. If she'd strangled herself."

"Jesus," Blackjack said, "the heat's too much for you white boys."

Tracy clutched her own throat, her hand upside down. "I see what you mean. But why? Scratch that question. I have a feeling I don't want to know."

Eric leveled his eyes on Blackjack. "It's simple, unfortunately. Angel knew she'd be forced to talk eventually, so she made a deal with Blackjack here. She'd tell him where the weapons were and split it with him later. In the meantime they'd perform their little act for us, fake a map, and all would be well. Only Angel had no intention of splitting with him. She came back to kill all three of us, but especially him."

"Come on, Eric," Tracy said. "You're scaring me."

"Sorry, Trace, but it's true. Blackjack is still an amateur at this kind of thing, but Angel's been dealing in deceit and double-crossing for years. She knew I'd never believe she talked unless there was some physical damage. Some cuts and bruises. I suspect she talked Blackjack into hitting her, but he couldn't keep at it as much as she wanted. So she made some bruises of her own. There's a lot more power in the grip upside down when you're choking yourself." He smiled at Blackjack. "How am I doing, Doc?"

261

Blackjack returned the smile, but there was a sadness in his eyes that made him look ill. He drew his .38 from the shoudler holster and pointed it at Eric. "You're the most irritating white man I've ever met." He waved at his crew behind him. "Pack it up folks. They know."

Tracy sagged. "I knew I wouldn't like it."

"Sorry, Tracy. But I warned you what I was at the beginning. I said I was a pirate, but you chose to interpret that to mean some kind of gentleman robber." He shook his head bitterly. "I don't have time to be a gentleman anything anymore. I'm dying. But before I go, I'm getting some of what's mine."

"What's yours? What the hell do you want?" Tracy demanded. "Guns, food, women? What?"

He gave her a hard look. "Not *things.* I want to live the way I want, for me. Hell, I'm not going to make some movie speech for you. I don't owe you an explanation."

"What are you going to do?"

He climbed to his feet, joined his crew. "I'm going to leave you here. We'll take your weapons and leave them a couple miles from here. I'll leave one of my armed crew to keep you covered while we get a good head start toward where the guns really are. You stay away from us and you'll live. That's all you get."

Eric looked at his watch again. "What about our ride to Santa Barbara?"

"Eric, never mind!" Tracy said.

Blackjack frowned at Eric. "Don't push it, Eric."

Eric's smile spread wider across his face. "Tracy, what do you know about the zoo in Hearst Castle?"

"I know there's got to be a point."

"Trust me."

"Somehow that doesn't make me feel better." Tracy shrugged. "The zoo. Hearst loved animals. Even when the field mice threatened to destroy his fruit trees, he hesitated to do anything about it because he didn't want them killed. That ought to clue you in on the way he felt about animals. He had two thousand fenced acres for what was once the largest private zoo in the country. He had something like thirty species of carnivores, including tigers and an elephant, and seventy species of assorted animals which he allowed to roam wherever they wanted. That enough?"

Eric shook his head.

She sighed. "He also had elaborate bear pits, lion pens, monkey houses. The whole thing was designed to provide maximum comfort for the animals. Kind of nice, when you think about it." She looked back and forth between Eric and Blackjack, who were staring at each other. "Th-th-that's all, folks."

Blackjack looked worse. His shoulders sagged under some invisible weight. His face was drawn, his eyes sallow.

"Unlike Tracy, Blackjack, I believed you

when you told us you were a pirate. Which meant there was no reason I should trust you when you took Angel away last night. I followed you, figuring if you did make a deal with her, you wouldn't be satisfied unless she personally showed you where the guns were hidden. And she did."

"How could she?" Tracy asked. "Unless . . ."

"Unless they were hidden at Hearst Castle. Exactly. A perfect place for the government to take them. Easy to defend if they had to, hard to get to. Only that five-mile road, which is now underwater."

"The zoo!" Tracy said suddenly. "They hid them in the zoo."

"Right. The animals were all gone, but they built a special bin under the bear pit, impossible to find unless you know it's there. If only BeBop knew what he was sitting on."

"But he never will," Blackjack said, his voice tired. "We'll go back, take them to the ship, and return to Liar's Cove to auction off whatever we don't keep. We'll make a fortune in goods."

Tracy dug her cane into the ground and struggled to her feet. "Do you know the kind of scum you'll be giving guns to?"

"He knows," Eric said.

"Not giving," Blackjack smiled. "Selling."

"Not selling, either, I think," Eric said, tapping his watch crystal. "I mean, you didn't think I'd follow you to the cache and then fall for this gag of luring us away, did you?"

Blackjack looked confused, then horrified.

He looked over his shoulder at Hearst Castle. "God, no!"

"God, yes," Eric said coldly.

The explosion lifted rocks and dirt and trees and concrete into a tangled plume of smoke and fire. Several smaller explosions followed, peppered with the chattering of boxes of bullets detonating like firecrackers. Bits of debris fell lazily to the ground as smoke swirled upward to join the Halo.

Blackjack spun angrily to face Eric, his jaw clenched, his lips trembling with rage. His dark skin seemed somehow even darker now. He thrust his .38 into Eric's face. "You made a terrible misjudgment thinking I wouldn't kill you for that."

Eric was calm, his features hammered in steel. "I didn't know whether you'd kill me or not, Blackjack. I'd like to think you wouldn't. But I wasn't willing to rely on faith. I've been wrong about people before."

Blackjack thumbed the hammer of his gun back with a deadly click. "Make it fast."

"After I followed you and Angel to the cache, I managed to make a fair time bomb out of all the stuff I found there. But first I moved some of it. Hid it."

Blackjack pressed the gun against Eric's forehead. "Where?"

"Well, now, that's the secret. There's not much hidden, though. Some rifles, pistols, a few boxes of ammunition. Not enough to conquer California, but enough for a few trained people on a floating farm, with a little luck, to protect themselves against any invasion. Maybe even move safely back to the land."

Blackjack stared at Eric for a full minute, maybe longer. Tracy held her breath, the rest of the crew shifted nervously.

Finally, Blackjack eased the hammer down on the gun, shoved it back into his holster. "Hell, what's a few blown up guns between good buddies like us? Hardly enough to justify me wasting a bullet on you"—he grinned—"this time."

20.

The Argo dropped anchor near the coast of what once was Santa Barbara. A few crumbled homes and stores clung to the cliffs and ridges, but the rest of the city had slid into the ocean in less than thirty seconds several months earlier. A few items marked the trail: a telephone pole sticking out of the side of the cliff, its wires running straight down into the ocean; the front end of a Dodge Omni teetering over the edge of a ridge, held back by a movie theater marquee that had pinned the back end to the street. The movie marquee read, CL N   EASTWO D IN . . .

Eric dropped his backpack over the side of the ship into the dinghy. Tracy handed her bow and quiver down to the young Australian man who would row them ashore.

"Where's Blackjack?" she asked.

Eric pointed and laughed. Blackjack was hoisting up his ratty skull and crossbones flag.

Tracy did not laugh. "Do you think he would

have killed us back there?"

"I don't know."

"I like to think he wouldn't have."

"Me too."

"Still, I'm glad you hid those guns."

He smiled at her. "Me too."

Tracy felt the weight of the Smith & Wesson .357 Combat Magnum in her waistband and patted it happily. Eric balanced his crossbow over one shoulder. His new Remington .32 was fully loaded with an eight-shot clip and tucked into his boot. An extra box of cartridges was stashed in his backpack.

Blackjack marched over with a huge grin and gestured at his flag. "Long may she wave, eh?"

"You too," Eric said, offering his hand.

They shook, Blackjack taking Eric's hand in both of his. They nodded at each other as if in agreement, not to something they said, but in acknowledgment of what they were.

"Come here," Tracy said, pulling Blackjack down to her level. She kissed him quickly, leaving one of her tears on his cheek.

Blackjack watched them climb into the dinghy. "Take care of him," he said to Tracy. "He has a bit of the pirate in him too."

"A bit too much," she said and waved.

The Australian rowed the dinghy across the orange-tinted water, the only sounds now were the screaming of sea gulls and the splashing of his oars. Eric was staring at the shore, his mind already locked on Timmy and the search for Fallows.

From the deck of *The Argo*, Blackjack watched the dinghy land on the narrow strip of beach. Eric hopped out, standing waist-deep in the water. He slipped into his backpack, handed Tracy his crossbow and her cane, and cradled her in his arms. His feet kicked up waves of water as he carried her to the shore.

Slowly, meticulously, they climbed the cliff, Eric helping Tracy when necessary, keeping an eye on her while pretending not to. Blackjack smiled. He had treated her wounds. Except for the hip, the rest were superficial. The cuts and gouges she'd received from Angel would heal in four to six weeks. They both were pretty battered up. Yet somehow they looked stronger than he'd ever seen them. Tougher.

"Brad's back," one of his crew shouted as the dinghy was raised back into place. "Should he weigh anchor?"

"Not just yet," Blackjack said, leaning over the railing, still watching.

It took another half hour for them to struggle up the face of the cliff. They rested for a moment. Eric said something. Tracy playfully swatted at him with her cane. They kissed.

Eric pulled Tracy to her feet. They marched into the thick brush, Tracy limping next to Eric. For a moment, he thought he saw them pause and wave at him. He wasn't sure, it could have been the rustling of the trees, a frightened bird. But he waved back, just in case.

THE SURVIVALIST SERIES
by Jerry Ahern

#1: TOTAL WAR   (960, $2.50)
The first in the shocking series that follows the unrelenting search for ex-CIA covert operations officer John Thomas Rourke to locate his missing famly—after the button is pressed, the missiles launched and the multimegaton bombs unleashed . . .

#2: THE NIGHTMARE BEGINS   (810, $2.50)
After WW III, the United States is just a memory. But ex-CIA covert operations officer Rourke hasn't forgotten his family. While hiding from the Soviet forces, he adheres to his search!

#3: THE QUEST   (851, $2.50)
Not even a deadly game of intrigue within the Soviet High Command, and a highly placed traitor in the U.S. government can deter Rourke from continuing his desperate search for his family.

#4: THE DOOMSAYER   (893, $2.50)
The most massive earthquake in history is only hours away, and Communist-Cuban troops, Soviet-Cuban rivalry, and a traitor in the inner circle of U.S. II block Rourke's path.

#5: THE WEB   (1145, $2.50)
Blizzards rage around Rourke as he picks up the trail of his family and is forced to take shelter in a strangely quiet Tennessee valley town. But the quiet isn't going to last for long!

#6: THE SAVAGE HORDE   (1243, $2.50)
Rourke's search for his wife and family gets sidetracked when he's forced to help a military unit locate a cache of eighty megaton warhead missiles. But the weapons are hidden on the New West Coast—and the only way of getting to them is by submarine!